Charles Du Hays

The Percheron Horse

Translated from the French of Charles Du Hays

Charles Du Hays

The Percheron Horse
Translated from the French of Charles Du Hays

ISBN/EAN: 9783337195380

Printed in Europe, USA, Canada, Australia, Japan

Cover: Foto ©Andreas Hilbeck / pixelio.de

More available books at **www.hansebooks.com**

THE

PERCHERON HORSE.

TRANSLATED FROM THE FRENCH

OF

CHARLES DU HUŸS,

AUTHOR OF THE "DICTIONARY OF THE PURE RACE;" "TROTTERS;" "THE BOOK
OF THE RACES;" "THE MEELEEAULL;" "THE HORSE-BREEDER'S GUIDE;" ETC.

ILLUSTRATED.

NEW YORK:

ORANGE JUDD & COMPANY,

245 BROADWAY.

LOVEJOY, SON & CO.,
ELECTROTYPERS & STEREOTYPERS,
15 Vandewater Street, N. Y.

TABLE OF CONTENTS.

—◆◆◆—

INDEX.

4

PREFACE.

The little volume which is now presented to the notice of the lovers of the horse in America is a translation of the work of a distinguished French author, who, holding a high position of trust, made this as a report to the Government. His views in some respects may be regarded as extreme, but on the whole they are characterized by strong common sense and are supported by a practical familiarity with all the phases of his subject which should give them weight.

The Percheron horse no doubt stands first among the draft breeds of the world. His value has been thoroughly tested in this country, and the fact is established beyond a cavil that with careful breeding, and probably an occasional renewal by the importation of fresh blood, the Percheron maintains his superior characteristics, and impresses them upon his descendants of only one-quarter or one-eighth blood to a very marked degree. The value of fast trotters, their encouragement by Agricultural Societies, and the enormous prices which have been paid for animals valuable simply for their speed as trotters, has no doubt had a tendency to direct the aims of horse breeders in a wrong direction. The result is, from whatever cause it comes, that the true horse-of-all-work has been neglected. The Percheron, combining as he does a certain attractive-

5

ness of style, very free action, considerable speed united
to power, with astonishing strength for his weight, and the
greatest kindness and docility, seems to offer to American
horse breeders an exceedingly useful animal, either to be
maintained distinct, or used for improving our stock of
both light and heavy draft-horses by crossings. The value
of this work, however, does not consist in its recommenda-
tion of this breed, or demonstration of its value in France,
but its bold discussions of the principles of breeding as applied to the improvement of the Percherons, and equally
applicable to that of other draft breeds, will doubtless
commend themselves to the careful consideration of
breeders.

Interest in the Percherons has increased greatly of late.
Several notable importations have been made, and excellent representatives of this noble breed are to be found in
the Eastern, Western, and Middle States. The engravings which embellish this volume are portraits of animals
owned by Mr. W. T. Walters of Baltimore, Md., through
whose interest in this subject the Publishers were induced
to issue this translation of M. Huÿs work.

THE PERCHERON HORSE.

PRODUCTION, REARING, AND IMPROVEMENT OF THE PERCHERON HORSE.

> . . . . *Facilis descensus Averno;*
> *Sed revocare gradum?*

Amost everything that has been written about the horse may be reduced pretty much to,—complaining that there does not exist a breed which unites, in an elevated degree, high moral to physical qualities; modestly seeking, and teaching the means of obtaining such a breed.

It is reasonable that such sentiments should surprise us, herein the heart of France, where, for a long time, a race of horses has flourished which may be said to fill the requirements proposed in every way.

The proof of this statement is easy: a hasty sketch of the principal characters of the breed suffices to furnish it.

To no ordinary strength, to vigor which does not degenerate and to a conformation which does not exclude elegance it joins docility, mildness, patience, honesty, great kindness, excellent health, and a hardy, elastic temperament. Its movements are quick, spirited, and light. It exhibits great endurance, both when hard worked, and when forced to maintain for a long time any of its natural gaits, and it possesses the inestimable quality of moving fast with heavy loads. It is particularly valuable for its

7

astonishing precocity, and produces by its work, as a two-year-old, more than the cost of its feed and keep. Indeed, it loves, and shows a real aptness for labor, which is the lot of all. It knows neither the whims of bad humor, nor nervous excitement. It bears for man, the companion of its labors, an innate confidence, and expresses to him a gentle familiarity, the fruit of an education for many generations in the midst of his family. Women and children from whose hands it is fed, can approach it without fear. In a word, if I may dare speak thus, *it is an honorable race.* It has that fine oriental gray coat, the best adapted of all to withstand the burning rays of the sun in the midst of the fields—a coat which pleases the eye, and which in the darkness of the night allowed the postilion of former times to see that he was not alone—that his friend was making his way loyally before him. It is exempt, (a cause of everlasting jealousy among the breeders of other races,) always exempt from the hereditary bony defects of the hock, and where it is raised, spavin, jardon, bone spavin, periodical inflammation, and other dreaded infirmities are not known even by name.

This truly typical race would seem a myth did it not exist in our midst. But every day we see, every day we handle this treasure,—the munificent gift of Providence to this favored region, to cause agriculture, that "nursing mother," to flourish, and with agriculture, peace and abundance.

I need not name this breed; every one from his incomplete sketch has recognized the fine race of steady and laborious horses, bred in the ancient province of Perche, (so justly entitled *Perche of good horses,*) plowing in long furrows the soil of Beauce, and thence spreading itself over all France, where its qualities render it without a rival for all the specialties of rapid draft.

Hence it is that all our provinces envy us the possession of the race, and even foreign countries seek after it with an eagerness amounting to a passion.

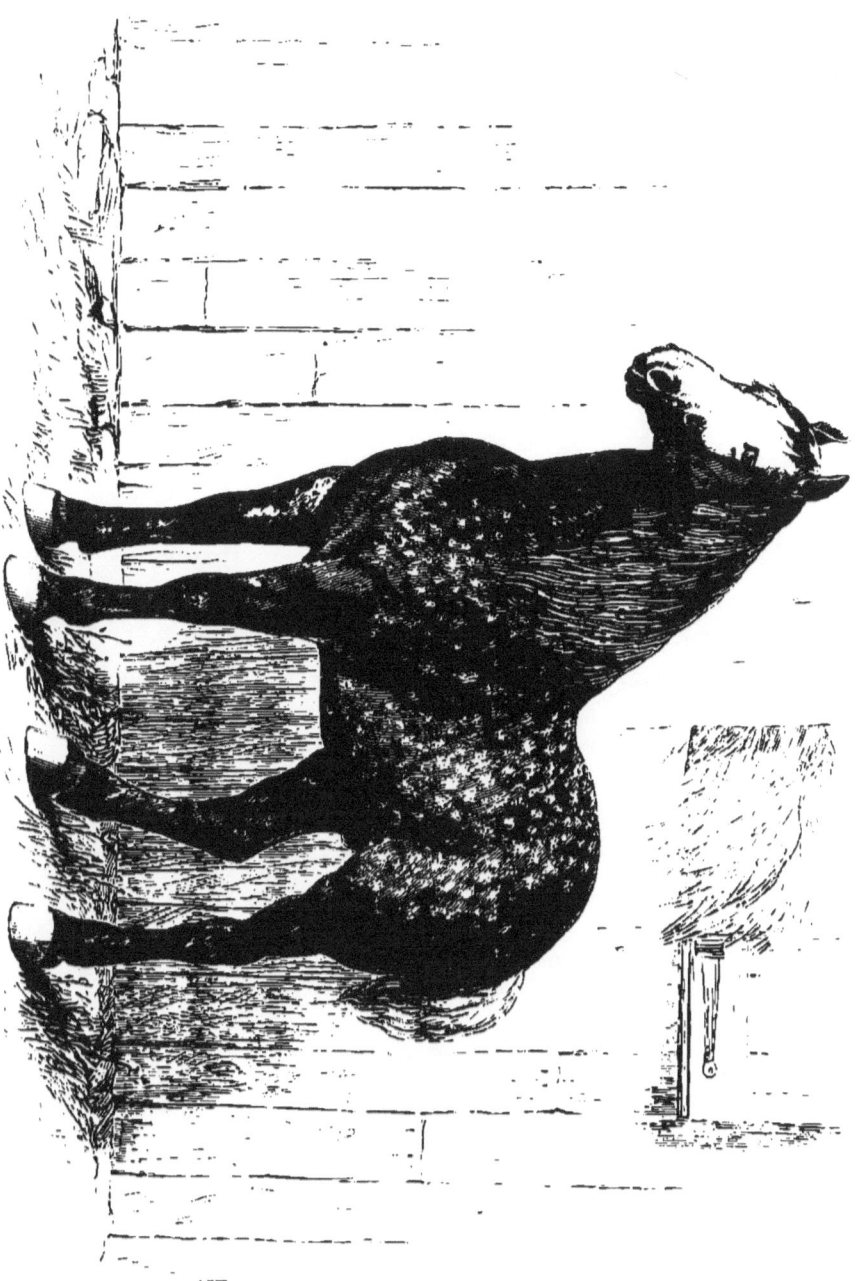

HERCULES.

The breeder,—who is ordinarily a farmer, not sufficiently rich to be beyond temptation,—finds himself without strength, without resistance in presence of this urgent demand. The finest types, not only of the males, but of the females also, are disappearing every day.

This, tending incessantly to deprive Perche of that in which it is so superior, is so much more to be dreaded as the question of filling up the vacancies and of saving this race from a tendency to degeneration and from inevitable destruction becomes the necessary corollary of such commercial operations.

Entered upon this course, if Perche does not adopt, without delay, salutary measures, if it does not make a vigorous effort to place itself in a condition, either to resist the tendency or to contribute to it in a well-maintained and uniform manner, the breed is fated to a complete eclipse at the moment even when the future belongs to it.

Indeed *the future* does belong to the Percheron horse, if he can sustain himself in the first rank of the truly useful races until the not far distant day when that era of triumph will come. Every thing now seems to incline to establish the truth of what, at first, appeared a paradox.

I am aware that, for the moment, the Percheron has, in the class of fancy-horses, an antagonist that seems to derive formidable strength from the prestige belonging to elegance. The English thoroughbred and its congeners are in possession of the scepter of fashion and "*bon-ton.*" But this antagonism, more apparent than dangerous, on account of the elevated but rather limited spheres in which it exists, will last but for a time, and will yield before reason and the necessities of a difficult situation.

Our age, factitious to excess, is governed by the demands and temptations of a luxury which is tending to ruin the most solidly established families. It wildly suffers patrimonies and fortunes to dwindle away under the lead of a vain and noisy ostentation, without perceiving

1*

that already they are decreasing and becoming less every day, under the continued action of the laws. A change will be brought about, and the effect of an inevitable reaction will be a return towards sobriety and simplicity.

Recovering from the intoxication of city luxury, the best minds will, let us hope, recover their tone in the quiet of the fields, and agriculture will regain its too long forgotten rights. Tired out by allowing themselves to be eaten up by that elegant guest called the fancy-horse, and by the army of evil-doing satellites following in his train, men will come back to the one which requires but little care, and which returns good service, to the one which does not object to work, the boon companion of every man desirous of following nature's law, which is that of labor.

The value of the Percheron is more evident than ever. It is this, among the serviceable races, which is called to the greatest fortune; for, of all the ordinary breeds, it is the nearest to the blooded, in shape and qualities. His usefulness causes him to be everywhere in demand. If the railroads have driven him from the highway, they claim him as an auxiliary in the centers of population and at all their termini; for he is eminently a trotter, remarkable for the ability to move at a relatively rapid gait, and excelling in the valuable faculty of rapid draft. Since the post-coaches have ceased to use these horses, the omnibuses of the large cities, and those communicating with the railroads, require increasing numbers.

This leads us to seek for the means of improving the Percheron race and of maintaining it in its original purity and perfection in the land of its birth. But let us first see what is the origin of this race, what country gave it birth, and by what characters it is to be recognized.

We have, for this examination, borrowed largely of those who have known and studied Perche intimately, and hope to remain truthful in following them step by step.

PART I.

GREATNESS AND DECLINE OF THE PERCHERONS.

————•♦•————

CHAPTER I.

GLÀNCE AT PÈRCHE.

The Department of Perche is too well known to need a description here. We will limit ourselves to the remark that this region, which has become so celebrated for its fine race of horses, represents an ellipse of about 25 leagues long by nearly 20 broad.

This ellipse is bounded on the north by Normandy; on the west, also by Normandy, and by Maine; on the east, by the portion of Beauce including Chartrain and Dunois; on the south, by the Vendomois—three portions of the ancient Orleanais.

At the present time, enclosed in the center of the four departments, Orne, Eure and Loir, Loir and Cher, and Sarthe, the territory of Perche comprises the following divisions:

1st.—The district of Mortagne (department of Orne);

2nd.—The district of Nogent-le-Rotrou, and a portion of those of Chartres, Dreux, and Chateaudun (department of Eure and Loir);

3rd.—All the western side of the district of Vendôme (department of Loir and Cher);

11

4th.—The eastern portion of the districts of Mamers and Saint Calais (department of Sarthe).

It is the summit region of the middle portion of the vast plateau extending between the sea and the basins of the Loire and the Seine. It is here that the rivers Sarthe, Huisne, Eure, Loire, Iton, Höene, Braye, Avre, Commanche, and Percheron Orne, take their source, springing up from the same plateau and crossing it on their way to the Channel and the ocean.

The country is, in general, uneven and hilly, cut up in every direction by small valleys watered by springs or small brooks flowing into the rivers above named. All these valleys, no matter of what extent, are natural meadows, and the most of them rich and fertile. But drainage could here be usefully applied everywhere, to rid them of their surplus humidity, and to purge them of their too abundant aquatic plants. The finest valley is that watered by the Huisne, which is second to none in France for length, extent, richness, and beauty of sites. Here are situated Nogent-le-Rotrou, Condé, Regmalard, Boissy, Corbon, Mauves, Pin-la-Garenne, Reveillon, etc., etc.,—all centers renowned for the beauty of their horses.

The land is generally clayey, lying upon a calcareous subsoil of the secondary formation. Some portions are silicious, the high and hilly points always so.

The Percheron country contains rather few meadows, in proportion to the total surface of the soil, and to this circumstance, probably, is due the superiority of its horses. Here the rearing takes place in the stable and the broodmare is found under the hand of the breeder. The idea of making use of her comes naturally to his mind. He works and feeds her well. All the secret of his breeding lies in these few words.

Here, for many years, agriculture has flourished; artificial meadows are everywhere cultivated with success, and are necessary to produce the enormous quantity of fodder consumed by the number of horses raised.

Among the plants for green and dry forage, clover first and then fenugreek are the favorites of the Percheron farmer. He uses plaster and marl with care, and would tell you, should the opportunity offer, that it is through system and superior cultivation that Perche has been able hitherto to meet the large demands made upon her from the commencement of the present century, particularly for the last fifty years. He is, moreover, laborious and persevering. Disregarding the industrial arts, the glory of other districts, his true vocation, his favorite occupation, is cultivating the ground and raising horses, which he has practised with zeal from the most remote period. In fact cannot this be inferred, even from the example of his early lords? The Counts of Perche, those old Rotrous, triple knights, had they not adopted as an emblem of their nobility the stamp of their horses' feet? . . . Not content with a single chevron, they placed three upon their standards, to signify both the superiority of their horses, and their infinite number. For in symbolical language (and none is more so than that of heraldry,) the number three implies infinity; and the oval form of the eastern courser's foot, to which the chevron is distinctly traced, was used in early times as a sign of chivalry, replacing the ancient ring of Rome. Hence comes, as a distinctive mark of nobility, the large number of coats of arms with chevrons, among those of the knights. The simple chevron was the designation of the noble, and the particular marks which often accompanied the chevron served to recall some exploit, some distinguished feat of arms, the nature of the tastes, or the possessions of the warrior who bore this blazon.

Perche is very much cut up: the farms generally small; the fields, likewise small and mostly enclosed by hedges. The temper of the Percheron breeder is invariably mild. He knows all the importance of attention to the race which he rears, and nevertheless, it must be confessed, that with the exception of the mildness with which he treats it, he has done next to nothing to ameliorate it or preserve it in its beauty. Nature, time, and the climate, have done all.

Perche has a climate eminently favorable to horse-breeding. Under its influence, the water is tonic and the food nutritious, the air is pure, bracing, and drier than that of Normandy. The sea is farther off, and its influence, in consequence, is less felt.

However, these can be but general attributes, for the country varies in aspect according to the district. The portion near Normandy, which is watered by the Sarthe, is much the same as that province. The grasses are, however, sparser, and especially do not have that extreme sweetness and great tonic quality which distinguish those of the environs of Courtomer and Merlerault, situated only a few leagues from the limits of Perche.

On the side of Beauce, there are vast plains sometimes undulating, and having much similarity to that province.

On the Maine side, the country gradually assumes the characteristics of aspect and cultivation peculiar to it, so that the transition between these two provinces is not an abrupt change, but they blend like the tones of a picture. Upon some points woods, ponds in the north-east, forage and grain upon the remainder, are the chief features, and are the sources of the revenues of the country.

CHAPTER II.

SKETCH OF THE PERCHERON RACE.

The height of the Percheron horse is generally $14^2|_4$ to 16 hands; he is of a sanguine temperament, mixed in variable proportions with the musculo-lymphatic; his color is almost always gray, and is, among the characteristic features, that which first strikes the eye.

According to their predominence, these temperaments constitute varieties which may be thus classed:

1st.—The light Percheron, in which the sanguine temperament predominates;

2nd.—The draft Percheron, in which the lymphatic temperament is the most fully developed;

3rd.—The type intermediary between these two, partaking of the one by its lightness, and of the other by its muscular force.

The latter is the most numerous, but it has much degenerated of late years; and there is a tendency to its disappearance since the post-coach service, which formed it, has gradually given way to other means of conveyance. It has style, although the head is rather large and long; nostrils well open and well dilated; eye large and expressive; forehead broad; ear fine; neck rather short, but well filled out.; whithers high; shoulder pretty long and sloping; breast rather flat, but high and deep; a well-rounded body; back rather long; the croup horizontal and muscular; tail attached high; short and strong joints, and the tendon generally weak; a foot always excellent, although rather flat in the low countries and natural meadows; a gray coat; fine skin; silky and abundant mane. Such are the most general characteristics of the old Percheron race. These are the points which are still noticed upon what remain of some old horses, preserved from the transformation which commenced long ago; for at the present moment everything is much changed. Since the time of the foreign crossings, the foot has become flatter, the head overcharged, the tendon still weaker, the back longer, the shoulder has lost its direction, and the croup has become shorter. The race has changed suddenly to fill new wants which have unexpectedly sprung up.

Of course these different characters are modified by the varieties upon which they are noticed, but the "*ensemble*" presents a striking similarity.

The light Percheron, suited to harness, is found particularly in the Norman portion, in the district of Mortagne, near Courtomer, Moulins-la-Marche, Aigle, Mesle-sur-Sarthe, and especially in the parishes of Mesnière, Bures, and Champeaux-sur-Sarthe. This is easily accounted for, as here is the best blood of France, near the region where has been found the best Norman type. Here the soil, temperature, and pasturage, are pretty near the same.

In going from Nogent-le-Rotrou to Montdoubleau, and following the limits of Perche-Manceau, by Saint-Calais, Vilvaye, Ferté-Bernard, Saint-Corme and Mamers, we travel over the birth-place of the heavy draft-horse. Here we meet with the heavy brood-mares.

In the center of Perche, at Mauves, Regmalard, Lougny, Corbon, Courgeon, Reveillon, Villiers, and Saint-Langis, nothing is bred; the farmer brings up the horse colts of Eperrais, Pin-la-Garenne, Coulimer, Saint-Quentin, Buré, Pervercheres and the breeding parishes of the district of Mortagne, Nogent-le-Rotrou, Montdoubleau and Courtalin.

Horses of different sexes and ages are never mingled in Perche; they are there separated with care. But it is not exactly the same in respect to kinds.

The post-coach and the heavy-draft horse are there to be met with upon the same ground. The post-coach horse is, to be sure, bred a little everywhere; his temperament and the conditions in which he is placed, prepare him for this specialty.

It is, as we see, at the two extremities of the ellipse (especially where the pasture grounds are), that the mares are found. In the center, at Mauves, Regmalard, Lougny, etc., etc., the inhabitants turn their attention to bringing up the colts.

CHAPTER III.

ORIGIN OF THE PERCHERON.

What, now, is the origin of the Percheron? Some attribute to him an Arabian ancestry; others, less explicit and without positively assigning to him so noble an origin, hold him to be strongly impregnated with Arabian blood. M. Eugene Perrault, one of the most extensive and skillful dealers in fancy horses in all Europe, has frequently remarked to me that of all the various races of horses none were so interesting to him as the admirable Percheron, and that, judging from his appearance and qualities, he was satisfied he was a genuine Arab, modified in form by the climate and the rude services to which he had for ages been subjected.

We cannot, however, find in history the written positive proof that the Percheron is an Arab, but we believe it easy, by fair historical deduction, to prove what he is in fact.

It is well known that after the defeat of the famous Saracen chief Abderame by Charles Martel, on the plains of Vouille, the magnificent cavalry of the foe fell into the hands of the victors, since more than 300,000 infidels were killed on that day, and the horses which they rode were, like themselves, from the East. Upon a division of the spoil a large number of these were assigned to the men of La Perche, of Orleanais, and Normandy, who composed the bulk of the French forces, and they must necessarily have left in their progeny indelible traces of their blood.

La Perche, like all Christian countries, furnished, as is well known, her contingent of fighting men to the crusades, and the chronicles cite several Counts of Bellesmer, Mortagne, and Nogent, barons and gentlemen of that province, who, with many of their vassals, made pilgrimages to the Holy Land.

The Abbe Faet, in a letter addressed to the Congress of Mortagne, July 16, 1843, and in his great work upon La Perche, cites in this connection a lord of Montdoubleau, Geffroy IV., and Rotrou, Count of La Perche, as having brought back from Palestine several stallions, which were put to mares, and the progeny most carefully preserved. The small number of the sires, their incomparable beauty, and manifest superiority, must have led to the *in-and-in* breeding so much deprecated by most breeders; but the qualities of the sires became indelibly fixed upon their progeny.

The lord of Montdoubleau was, it is said, the most zealous of the advocates and breeders of the new blood, and, being the most zealous, was the most successful; hence it is that the Montdoubleau stock is to this day the best in Perche. The Count Roger, of Bellesmer, imported both Arabian and Spanish horses, as did Goroze, the lord of Saint Cerney, Courville, and Courseroult; these are historical facts which have their importance. Like chronicles, it is true, exist for other provinces—for Limousin, for Navarre, for Auvergne (the land of noble horses), also for Brittany and Maine; but in the latter not the least sign of Eastern blood is perceptible. The fact is, the crusaders from all the French provinces naturally brought back with them more or less of the Eastern blood, which they had learned to appreciate on the plains of Palestine—but the truth is, it has not been preserved elsewhere; and that we in La Perche, after so many centuries, should be so fortunate as to be able to show the traces of it, should stimulate us to its careful preservation.

From the time of the Roman domination, the horse in his oriental forms was not only valued by the Gauls, but was particularly prized in Perche. In 1861 a subterranean vault was discovered in the middle of a field, near Jargeau (Loiret), upon the borders of Perche. It contained a statue of Bacchus, surrounded by bacchanals, with which were found a horse, a stag, a boar, some fish, a grape vine, and other native products of the country; but the horse was indubitably of the Arab form, which goes to prove, either that at that remote period there were Arabians in the country, or that the native local race from which the portrait was taken resembled the Arabian.

These historical data, these inductions, incomplete as they may be, lead to the belief that for antiquity the Percheron yields to no other of our French races, and that the soil which has nourished and preserved it, must be one of the best in France for horse breeding.

Under the feudal rule and inhabited by tenants ever at war, Perche must always have been an equestrian country, and the horse must have been there in every age the companion of man. He must have been really a first class necessity. In those times of continued war and hostile surprises, what property was more movable and so easily taken to a place of safety? How glorious the possession of such noble coursers, and like the Rotrous, to own more than could be counted, as was proudly shown by the heraldic chevrons upon their broad banners, displayed from the towers of Mortagne and Nogent!

But had the Percheron then, as a race, the characteristics it now possesses? This is not probable; it must have been lighter, but still possessing within itself the character which it now presents. The essential point is to prove that there was, at that period, a native race; and if the extraordinary life formerly led there—if the aspect of the country, which must have been always fertile—if the historical inductions do not prove it—the universal tradition of the whole country should not leave us in any doubt in respect to the fact.

Let us, then, take no account of the silence of historians. This silence is no proof of the non-existence of the Percheron. Most of these writers were gentlemen of the equestrian order; they prized the saddle-horse, while they ignored the equally useful breeds of all work.

—◆◇◆—

CHAPTER IV.

MODIFICATIONS OF THE PERCHERON RACE.

The Percheron race comes from the Arab; but it is useful to know the causes which have separated it from the primitive type. How has it been modified? How has it lost the Arabian character, in which it must have been at first clothed? A large number of the French races have been even more profoundly modified, and have become abject, miserable, puny, and misshapen. All equine races have been changed by the effects of climate, by the extinction of the feudal system, and by the inauguration of peaceful habits which have made an agricultural and draft-horse of the horse primitively used for the saddle and for war. The Percherons must have been especially modified by contact with the breed of Brittany, where their striking characteristics are now met with in a large number of individuals.

However, it has been vigorously attempted to offset the intrusion of the heavy horse by the continued use of the Arabian horse. Indeed, we see, towards 1760, under the administration of the Marquis of Brigges, manager of the stud-stables of Pin, all the large number of fine Arabian, Barb, and eastern stallions, that this establishment owned, were put at the disposition of the Count of Mallart for use at his mare-stables of Cóèsme, near Bellesme. The arrival of the Danish and English stallions at the stud-stables of Pin put an unfortunate end to the influence of the Arab horse in Perche, and it will now be many a long year before the eastern blood will be seen as before. It is only towards 1820, still at the same chateau of Cóèsme, with the grandsons of those old admirers of the Arabians, that we find again two Arab horses. from the stud-stables of Pin, *Godolphin* and *Gallipoli*. These two valuable stock-getters, both gray, again gave tone and ardor to the Percheron race, and transformed definitely into gray horses the stock of the entire country, which had, it was said, become less uniform, and of all colors.

The Brittany horses have been strongly attracted towards Perche by the immense outlet offered by the public service, since the increase of the roads, to the Percherons. Mixtures between the two races must have been frequent. And when a good Brittany horse was there met with, he must have been made use of, and the old native type has gradually tended to disappear, and its traces become more and more rare. This mixture of Percheron and Brittany blood, too well marked to be questioned, arises from several causes, which we will take up successively in review.

CHAPTER V.

THE FIRST MODIFICATION, DUE TO CONTACT WITH THE BRITTANY RACE.

Perche is bounded, in its whole length, by the immense plains of Beauce. On account of this position, it was always traversed by the post-coaches for Paris, and by all the supplies that came from the West.

Being the intermediate point between the principal home of the Brittany draft-horse and the immense markets which Beauce and Paris offered, its territory was the necessary stopping-place of everything that came from

the West. It has been for many years the rendezvous of
the draft races of the whole West.

Now, see in what an exceptional position this country
is placed.. First and foremost, I do not hesitate to say
that there exists no French race which could have multiplied and preserved its original type under such unhappy
influences. We can but deplore the slight care taken in
preserving it pure and intact, and the want of judgment
in the delicate operation of crossing.

There has been no uniform and logical plan for improving as well as increasing it. To make the greatest possible
profit out of this hen with the golden eggs has been the
only aim.

When the post-coaches, wagon transportation, and the
public conveyances were organized and generalized; when
every thing requiring the use of the horse had undergone
excessive development; when the improvements of our
roads, the multiplicity of business transactions, and the
enormous internal traffic, required increased and rapid
locomotion, all eyes were turned towards Perche, and it
became necessary for her to satisfy the increased demand.

Let us see in what condition was the Percheron breeder
to satisfy all these demands. As for race, he possessed the
best. Strong, yet quick, it was that, of all others, which
contained the most blood. It owed this to the soil and
climate. It was the best to feed, the easiest to raise, and
the most favorably situated to be cheaply multiplied. And
with all this, it had at its door the best of known markets.

Wagons, diligences, and post-coaches, required horses
such as the Percheron cultivator loved to breed for himself.
Hence that sympathetic understanding which developed
itself more and more between the Percheron producer
and the consumer occupied in public transportation. And
the anxiety to meet the demand was one of the most active
causes of degeneration and of the drafts made upon this
and the neighboring breeds.

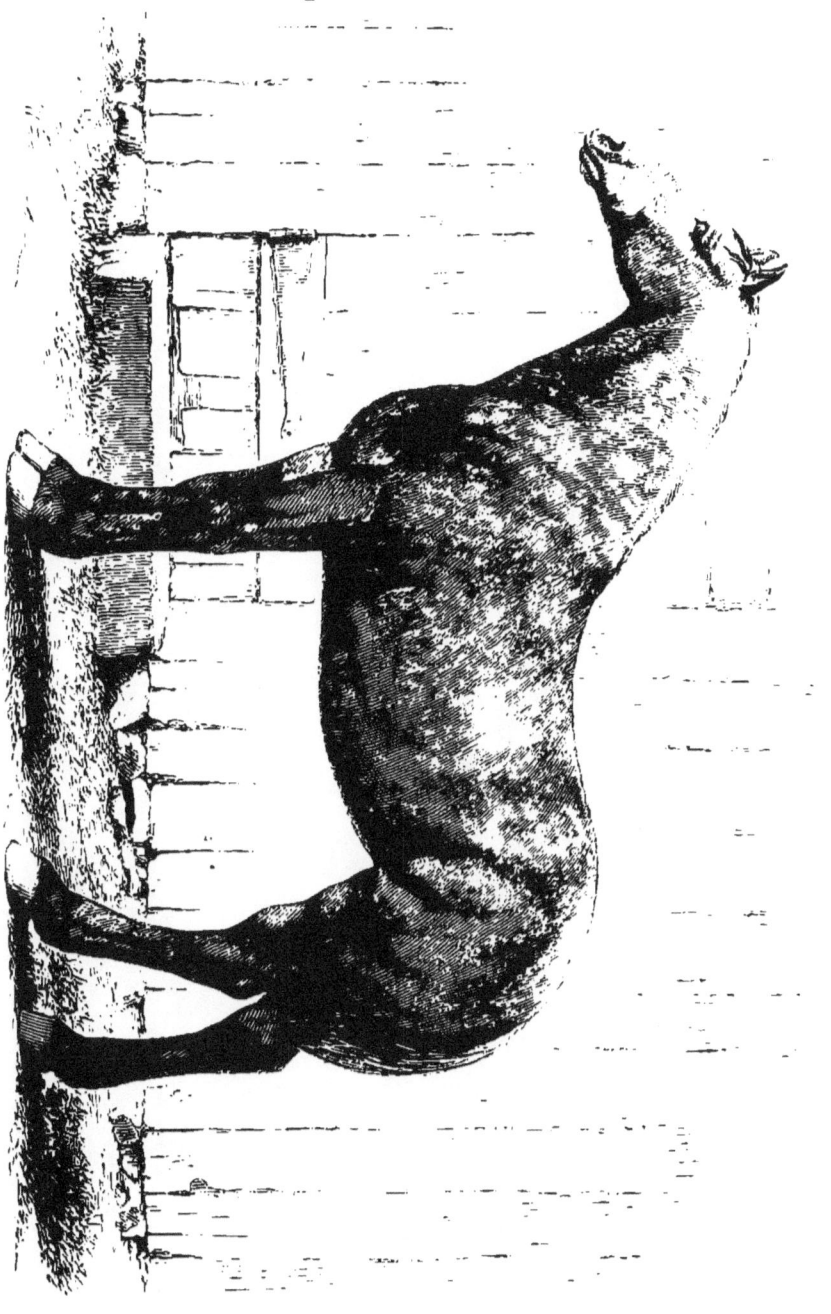

ALENE.—MARE.

CHAPTER VI.

CONDITIONS UNDER WHICH THEY ARE BRED.

We know how the sexes are divided in Perche; one section of the province produces, while another raises what the other has produced. No matter what may be the class to which she belongs, light or heavy, or partaking of both, the mare is expected to breed every year. If barren, she is sold, and this fault continuing, she passes into public use. During her gestation she works constantly. A few days of rest, before and after foaling, is the only time lost. The remainder of the time her work pays abundantly for her keep and the interest on her cost.

At the age of five or six months, the colt is abruptly weaned and sold. Its price varies from five to six hundred francs—sometimes more, but this is the exception—and so far it has cost nothing.

Led into the interior upon the fertile meadows of Mauves, Pin, Regmalard, Corbon, Lougny, Reveillon, Courgeron, Saint-Langis, Villiers, Courgeoust, etc., etc., it remains one year unproductive. In winter it is fed upon hay, in the stable, and during the fine season turned into the fields to graze. To sum up, it is rather poorly nourished on bran, grass, and hay.

The reason is, it is as yet unproductive to its master, and it feels the effects. Wait a little; its hardest time has gone by, and work will soon soften its lot. It reaches, in this manner, the age of 15 or 18 months. What has it cost for keeping? Very little. Estimate, about 80 or 100 francs. At this age it is put to work. Naturally docile and in the hands of a man always patient and mild, its training is generally easy. Assigned to farm labor, it plows or draws a wagon. Harnessed with four or five colts of its own age, together they pull what would be an easy load for two good horses.

Put before two oxen, or joined to three of its companions, it plows and is never overworked.

Now, it is better fed, and taken a great deal better care of. Its "*morale*" improves, and its master seems to delight in contemplating the progress and the development of its qualities. Thus, in traveling through Perche, one involuntarily stops in the midst of the fields to see it work, never tired of admiring the vigor it displays, and the gentleness with which it is treated.

The bait is there. At the age of three the Beauce farmer buys it to work his soft and light soil. For him, it must be preserved intact, its development uninjured, nay encouraged.

Master, servants, large and small, all deeply imbued with the love of the horse, unite in this work with admirable skill.

It has thus worked during one year, abundantly fed, but receiving little or no grain. Doing enough light work to pay for its keep, the master has received, besides its manure, a heavy interest on the cost, as we will presently see.

This premature work, which would have been injurious under a careless management, is, on the contrary, beneficial when it is in the hands of a good master. This is so much the general case, that the contrary is the exception. The animal grows and becomes better developed in size and strength.

Now, as we before observed, the Beauce farmer comes to buy. He lives in a country of proverbial richness. The work there is abundant, but the nature of the soil renders it extremely easy. The fields, very much divided, and distant one from another, make a rapid gait indispensable.

In Beauce, the horse cannot be replaced as a beast of burden; no matter how dear his keeping, his use is indispensable; the ox cannot be his competitor. But it is a fact of the greatest importance to state, that it is to the ox that the Percheron horse owes a part of his celebrity.

As is well known, Beauce is the exceptional country for cereals; the horse and sheep are pretty much the only animals which there produce a manure required by such husbandry. Add to this the breadth of land under tillage, and the extreme fertility of the soil, and the large number of horses kept by the Beauce farmer will be accounted for.

At three years old, the Percheron dealer sells his horse for 900 or 1,000 francs, and sometimes more, according to his merit. But he does this only in order to buy other colts; and the profit has been, in fact, sufficiently large to warrant him in this. He has had against him only the chances of mortality. These are small; the race is tough· and hardy. Accidents are more to be dreaded, and these sometimes occur. Living in the open air, in the company of other animals, the young colt is a little exposed to the influences of chance. But the fields are enclosed, the master's eye is upon it, and, to sum up all, the large profit covers every thing.

Reaching Beauce at three years old, he is subjected to hard work. The work is easy enough, but there is much of it. He must be quick, the breadth of land is very extensive, and the work must be done. Sowing and harvesting—these two words sum up the Beauceron agriculture. Otherwise expressed—plowing and hauling. As regards the horse, all must be done promptly and quickly.

But if he be hard worked, on the other hand, nothing is denied him. He eats as much grain and hay as he pleases. What difference does this make to the farmer? Do not his labor and his manure pay for his nourishment? And, moreover, how act otherwise? As we have seen, nothing can supply his place. Necessity has no law.

He lives in this way a year, with abundant food. Sometimes he succumbs; the mortality is quite large in this region. But the stock which remains after such a training

2

offers many guaranties to the the dealer who buys it to transfer, if they suit, to the express and omnibus companies; or if they belong to the draft race, to the contractors, wagoners, and builders, of Paris. At five, he is bought by the horse-dealer at the annual horse fair on St. Andrew's Day in the town of Chartres. There he is delivered, the farmer leading his horse upon the ground. The prices vary from 1,000 to 1,400 francs. The profit is small, sometimes nothing, the greatest gain being his work, which cannot be dispensed with. The feeble have perished; the survivors owe their lives only to their robust constitutions.

Before dedication to his final use, he has thus passed through four hands; all these have shared the risks of his rearing. The most serious have been for the last owner; but he was also the wealthiest, and to him also has he been the most useful.

Thus, we see, the foal costs almost nothing, and his work pays for his keep. Perfectly well fed, and exercised from his tenderest age, the Percheron has always been the first draft-horse in the world, and he would have constantly improved, if his admirable qualities themselves had not led to his degeneration.

CHAPTER VII.

CAUSES OF THE DEGENERACY OF THE PERCHERON HORSE.

The breeding of the Percheron horse has been so much the more stimulated, in consequence of his situation, his well-known qualities, and the favorable economical circumstances in which he is placed.

Was not everything in his favor? Sure and increasing sales and great facility in raising?

In a word, Perche is not large; the number of horses that it can produce is limited, and not being able to answer all the demands made upon it, competition stepped in.

At first, the finest types, the males especially, were sold. Then, little by little, the traffic increasing, the finest females, in their turn, commenced to appear upon the market.

The interior of France and foreign countries, Prussia especially, were anxious to possess them, the latter country, in order to form a race of draft-horses, which it absolutely needed, in consequence its own becoming too light.

It is the only race which has been accused of no faults, —simply because it has satisfied a real want and has been able to satisfy it fully.

The sale of colts becoming greater and greater, and all the farmers being interested in buying them to raise, Brittany sent hers upon the markets. They made their appearance in Perche and in the fairs of Mortagne, Courtalin, etc., etc., taking their place there alongside the colts of the country.

The breeding-mares being sought after, and in consequence sold, it became necessary to replace them. Their offspring sold too well not to think of increasing their number. Hence the introduction, at first, of a large number of Brittany mares, and afterwards of mares from Caux, Picardy, etc., etc., approaching nearest, both as to height and coat, to the race of the country.

If there had been among them only the Brittany mares, I would but half complain: these are well bred; and moreover, has not Perche contributed to the improvement of the Brittany race by sending into their country such famous stallions as *Pomme, Bijou,* and *Tancrede?* But the mares from Picardy, from Caux and from Boulogne—the scrofulous races of the North! What can be said for them?

This introduction is not of yesterday; it is already of long date. But it may be boldly advanced that it is only since 1830 that it has been effected upon a very large scale.

1830 was the era of the systematic infusion of the English pure-blood into our French half-blood races. Having become, by this fact, less fit for service, they commenced to lose their credit in the eyes of thinking men. The rich ran after the English, while others wanted the German horse, and this made the latter's fortune. The majority addressed themselves to Perche, and thus obliged her to multiply anew a stock already become insufficient.

In Upper Perche, that is to say, towards the Norman part, in the district of Mortagne, the introduction, (we are ignorant of its cause,—perhaps from the presence of some good stallions,) was not so great; but it did, nevertheless, take place, and its traces are discovered at every step. It would be very difficult, if not impossible, to find there at the present moment, a Percheron completely free from mixture of foreign blood.

CHAPTER VIII.

STARTING POINT OF THIS DEGENERATION.

As long as the post-coaches were flourishing and the diligences crossing France in every direction, it was especially a horse fit for their uses that Perche devoted itself to produce. But since these modes of transportation have been modified, the race, with them, has undergone a complete transformation. As this country only possessed, as an outlet for the light part of its stock, the expresses, omnibuses, and post-office services in the interior of Paris, and later the private post teams, etc., etc., which only employ quick-gaited horses, it became necessary to think of rendering the race heavier, in order to replace the monopoly of the mail stages and diligences by another monopoly. Had it not before it the necessity of satisfying the commercial wants—that is to say, the express cartage, the heavy work of the contractors and builders of Paris, and in the provinces, the services of the large towns, and the express and other business connected with all railroads? The fear of losing this important market offered to his qualities of speed, strength, and honesty, tempted the breeder to infuse too suddenly the blood of the heavy draft-horse. He might have accomplished this more slowly and gradually, by means of a rational coupling with the heaviest bodied native types; but our age, eager to enjoy, did not leave him the time. To answer to these new wants, Perche opened wide its doors to all the heavy mares that it could meet with. Many came from Brittany, others from Picardy and Caux, and some from Boulogne. During this time the ancient stallion of the country, eagerly sought after by all those who wished to create fine draft studs, passed into the interior and even into foreign countries.

The success of the Percheron race was very great. All the departments wished to acclimate it. The prices of these stallions had increased so rapidly in a few years, that they had tripled and quadrupled. Accordingly, the possessors sold them. The administrative authorities, aided by the élite of the proprietors, endeavored, however, to hinder this emigration. They formed a stud-stable at Bonneval; but this establishment was not composed of types that were homogeneous and adapted to assure a regular and continuous improvement. Prizes were given at Mortagne, Nogent-le-Rotrou, Illiers, and Vendôme. But an end was arrived at contrary to what was desired. The prizes served as signs to the dealers. Perche was visited to buy first-class horses. What surer guaranty than the prize? And then, how could the breeders resist the prices of 3,000 and 4,000 francs, and even more, offered the proprietor of a stallion?

It will be objected that these stallions, before disappearing, had already served; I know this. But how served? They had served at two or three years, before their complete development, and it was at the age at which they would have been most useful, that they were withdrawn from their district, and the same thing was true with the best mares.

Several departments carried off great numbers; they were sent everywhere. A great many proprietors bought them. Thus disappeared, gradually, the flower of the breeding-mares. The race was cut off in its prime. Perche stretched its sails to the winds of the present without thinking of the future!

Stallions of all kinds now came forward; stallions from Brittany, Picardy, Caux, and Boulogne. The heaviest were preferred. The change was so rapid, that, to-day, in many places, there does not remain the slightest trace of genuine Percheron blood. It is a mixture which betrays itself to the eye by coarse forms, foreign to the original type, and in the *morale* by a sensible loss of that generous spirit, and of that indescribable something that we so much admired. Perche would formerly have disowned stock lacking the eastern character; still, their presence is not without instruction. It gives the measure of the great climatic qualities of this province, and proves what it could have done with well-chosen animals.

Such is its force of assimilation, that after nourishing some generations upon its soil, it is able to reform them, and impart that sacred fire, and that build, which can only come from the nourishment of its hills.

The department authorities, unwearied by the slight success of their first attempts, renew their efforts, from year to year, to oppose the progress of this degeneration, and endeavor to combat it by the strongest measures.

The department of Eure and Loir, undeterred by the costly and disastrous failure of the Bonneval breeding stud, continues still its patriotic work, and keeps up its encouragements, in the form of prizes to stallions and broodmares—encouragements to which Orne and Loir, and Cher, appropriate annually considerable sums.

There was formed, some years ago, at Chateaudun, with the most disinterested and patriotic design, a powerful association of proprietors, known under the name of " *The Horse Association of Perche*," having for its mission the furnishing of good stallions to the farmers.

Trotting matches at Illiers, Courtalain, Vendôme, Mont-doubleau, and Mortagne, have been established; but, with all this, a success worthy of such efforts has not yet been obtained, on account of a lack of uniformity in the movement.

Competition at the fairs gives but too often the spectacle of *size* being systematically encouraged; while trotting, in consequence of the speed required, leads to the employment of English cross-breds. Would this operation were well directed! But even then, would this English blood be used in right proportions? I doubt it. When it is used, it is used too much; for, this blood, if it be not employed with extreme reserve, an extreme parsimony, if I may so speak, results in injuring the honest traits and the valuable quality of early maturity; it destroys, in fact, that precocity of the breed, which enables it at an early age to pay for its feed by its labor. The breeders are almost invariably small farmers, and they cannot afford to lose the time necessary to mature fancy horses; they must have quick sales and quick returns.

PART II.

OF THE MEANS OF REGENERATING THE PERCHERON HORSE.

Perche, in order to retain its best customers, and not drop to a level with the common herd of horse-breeders, must at once have recourse to systematic means of improvement. Her breeders have shown a deplorable alacrity in the downward course, which has brought upon them the depreciation in the value of their stock, of which they begin to perceive the effects.

> " Facilis descensus Averno ;
> Sed revocare gradum,
> Hoc opus, hic labor est !"

Unanimity of will and unity of means are both necessary to accomplish the ascent, and regain the position which the breed has lost. Two measures present themselves as each essential in accomplishing this result. The first step is to restore the disturbed equilibrium by a well-planned and uninterrupted series of crosses, effected within the breed. This would arrest the evil. The second step should be, subsequently, to breed up by improving crosses, practised with a wise and circumspect deliberation. This would be making progress.

At the very outset, and continued parallel with this course of breeding, a *Stud-book* should be instituted, in order that all thus subjected to systematic improvement should be brought together, and thus initiate a general improvement of the breed. The development of these ideas will furnish matter for the following chapters.

32

CHAPTER I.

REGENERATION OF THE PERCHERON BREED.

There are two ways of crossing applicable to any breed, both of which have had their earnest partisans. So much clamor has been made about them, I think, only because they have been simultaneously used and often mingled, and the results have been deranged by their use. This might have been avoided by commencing with the simplest and continuing with the best.

The first may be called the renewal of a breed within itself, or interbreeding; the second, improving by foreign blood. We will pass them rapidly in review, trying to reach in the results the solid basis of truth.

CHAPTER II.

REGENERATION OF THE BREED THROUGH ITSELF, OR BY SELECTION.

The first manner, also called *selection*, consists in making, among the race itself, a rational, judicious choice of the most perfect types; those which are as free as possible from the most prominent defects of the breed; those which best recall the primitive type, if it possess the superior qualities which it is required to reproduce; those which, healthy and vigorous, seem to have among themselves the most affinity. This choice ought to be severe and rigorous, nor should we be discouraged by the small number of the elect.

2*

From the issue of this first selection, make a similar choice, and with them and their progeny march persevering-ly in the same way, without ever looking to the right or to the left—that is to say, without ever listening to advice which would modify the work commenced, or to praises which might induce the desire for too rapid results. To proceed too fast is perhaps a still greater error than to stop on the way, inasmuch as it often renders a retro-grade movement obligatory and reduces to nothing the results of several years of success.

It is indispensable that the selections from which a good progeny is desired should be completely grown—that is to say, the horses should be at least four years past, and the mares fully three years old.

Sell, without remorse, to the trade the least successful types, and most carefully keep the good. The horses, after serving some campaigns in their adult age, can be sold without inconvenience; a few well-proved types are suf-ficient for a district. But never part with the mares when they are remarkable for their conformation, temper, aptitude to work, and for their qualities as breeders.

Thus, in order to keep the breeders clear of tempta-tions which are always dangerous, and as a good means of guidance, prizes become a question of life or death for the future of the race. It is, in fact, by means of prizes and rewards, liberally distributed for the class of mares of three to ten years inclusively, that they can be kept in the region. It is by awarding the prize at three years, after they have been covered, in paying at first but one-half of the prize and the remainder only after they have foaled and have been again covered, that they can be virtually controlled. After ten years, as they no longer meet with either a good or profitable sale, special encouragement may cease. Moreover, the breeder who during eight years has received in prizes a sum often superior to the money value of his mare, and recognizing that he possesses in her a brood-mare of merit, will no longer commit the folly of parting with her for a price which would be ridiculous.

There is such extreme delicacy in the manner of distributing these prizes, that I scarcely dare refer to it.

The members of the council-board, who have the appropriation for the prizes, should have naturally and rightfully the honor of awarding them. I would then wish, that in each district (what I am about to say excludes the public fairs, in which a jury, numerous, and consequently never unanimous in opinion, opposes the execution of a uniform idea), the council-board and the council of the district, charged at the same time with the establishment of the *Stud-book*, of which I will speak in a separate chapter, should be willing to accept this mission, which they would perform with the aid of the inspector-general of the Stud-stables. Each year, by their care, the mares of a district would be scrupulously examined and classed for the prize.

These premiums should be granted for eight years, to the best three-year-old fillies, to which this distinction would give the entrance upon the *Stud-book*. In the first year of the establishment of this book, destined to contain the genealogical documents relative to the celebrities of the race, the mares above three years, which have been found worthy to be inscribed, should be likewise given prizes, and this same should be allowed them as a pension up to the age of ten years.

These inducements should be annual, and kept up as long as the prize-mare is kept as a breeder and in proper condition, that is to say; sound of wind, and exempt from the glanders. Other blemishes, the natural consequence of work and age, might be tolerated.

Following the same system and conditions, similar prizes should be awarded to stallions, without paying attention to rewards which they may have received from other quarters. But as the resources of which a department disposes, augmented even by private contributions, are not inexhaustible, it is urgent that the prizes, always liberal and remunerative, being from two to four hundred francs for mares, and from four to eight hundred francs for stallions, should be accorded only to specimens of real merit. Quality, when it effects the regeneration of a race, is always preferable to quantity.

It is, especially, necessary to excite earnest breeders by all possible means, to preserve or to buy remarkable Percherons, presenting in their form and character the type of the stallion. And, if the prizes of four to eight hundred francs, of which we have just asked the institution, should not appear to the authorities of the departments a sufficient means to impart the necessary impulse for the complete success of this measure, the departments might themselves buy some remarkable types, and either use them, themselves, in gratuitously serving the finest mares, or in confiding them to good farmers, in whose hands they would be given the prize and used almost for nothing, as long as their health permitted them to be profitably kept. After a certain number of years these stallions might even become the property of their keepers, or they might, from the beginning, be granted them at reduced prices, with the obligation, on the one side, that they should be used with judgment and preserved with care, and on the other side, with the promise of a largely remunerative prize. Love of gain has driven the peasant to strip himself of everything he owned that was good; it now belongs to the authorities, by the incentive of gain, to induce this same peasant to pursue a wiser course.

Oppose as much as possible the use of stallions before fully four years old, and the fillies being put to breeding before reaching their third year. This can only be attained by giving the prize, in the class of fillies, to such as have been served at the age of three years, by stallions of at least four years old.

Crossing by selection has numerous advocates, and from all time, the best-informed, the most practical men, have been unanimous in proclaiming that *blood is only preserved and improved by blood*—that is to say, by selection. It is easy and not expensive, inasmuch as the necessary subjects are always at hand; it is natural, inasmuch as its simplicity is apparent to every mind. And, if it does not bring the rapid results so pleasing to those too eager for profit, it is, at least, always sure. For, without giving at first exceptional results, it never fails in its effects, by reason of the affinity existing between the different individuals, and by reason especially of their perfect conformity with the climate and soil. In fact, this conformity is not an indifferent matter, and it has been found by experience that animals, noted upon their native soil for their sureness in reproducing, and for the invariable transmission of their qualities to their descendants, frequently fail in these respects when imported into another country. Often, several years roll by before they recover that equilibrium of health and that tranquillity of animal functions, which permit them to reproduce in a sure, equal, and fixed manner, without which an improvement in the type cannot take place.

Selection has long been practiced in Perche, and it has there produced for a long time the best results, which were interfered with only by the importation from Picardy, Caux, and Boulogne, of animals of inferior blood.

Among the bovine species, we have curious examples of the value of selection, especially those furnished in Cotentin, where a breed exists the finest, best, and the most sought after in France. Crossing with foreign blood, which fashion, at one date or another, had wished to prescribe, has always been forbidden as a crime in this country. It is thus that the finest herds of La Manche, and especially those of M. Mannoury of Canisy near Saint-Lô have been formed. The success of this breeder began at Ebisey near

Caen, where he commenced a few years ago and where the stock can be easily examined.

A bull of the Cotentin race, the most perfect and best bred that could be found, put to heifers of the same breed, chosen among the finest types, was the starting point officially recorded. Selection, operating upon this progeny, as it had operated in the beginning, was continued without intermission, and, by these means it has produced a herd all the members of which are alike and constantly transmitting identical qualities.

CHAPTER III.

CONSANGUINITY.

Conjugal consanguinity has neither partisans nor friends. The physiologist, physician, priest, and legislator, have always launched against it the same anathema. All, in making war against it, knew that it was the surest method of establishing a fixed and permanent race; but, all, preoccupied in seeking a means of universal fusion, thought they had found in the prohibition of this a leveler destined to equalize everything.

It was feared that certain families would become too individualized, too marked in their tendencies; and all, without acknowledging it, endeavored to close a way which might lead to the engrossment of fortunes.

Close interbreeding, in the horse, has not the same political inconveniences; this is clearly apparent; but with us, the desire to legislate upon and regulate everything, reducing all to a common level, has prevailed. Equine consanguinity has not, any more than the other, found favor.

One fact, however, strikes any one at the outset who has

ANTHONY.

studied the equine races, followed, step by step, their progeny, and made himself acquanted with their performances. This fact is:

If a horse is remarkable over all others in one of the three following ways : personal beauty, high qualities, or sureness of reproduction; go back boldly to his origin, and you will find yourself, at each step, face to face with close interbreeding—that is to say, the reforming of a race by means of itself, the result of great qualities increased by drafts made at the source of a generous blood.

The thoroughbred race in England, which has been formed but with a very limited number of primitive agents, and which, consequently, soon became consanguine, has anew, and at two distinct epochs, absorbed in every degree and repeatedly the blood of two famous groups, represented, the first by *Byerly Turk*, *Darley Arabian*, and *Godolphin Arabian;* the second, by *Matchem*, *Herod*, and *Eclipse.* At the present moment, it maintains itself, thanks to a universal consanguinity, and everything good which exists, by going back inevitably to these sole progenitors, now forms but one and the same family. Magnificent results have come from these alliances, and every day it can be proved that this blood has not degenerated.

It is the same in all breeding countries, and it has been shown, (for proofs see the journal "*La vie à la campagne*", of the 30th November, 1863), that especially in Merlerault, the nursery of the fine French breeds, everything exceptionally good which exists, or which has existed, is the result of consanguinity—that is, " in-and-in breeding."

The following is the conclusion of the author of this note :

These examples (the pedigrees of the best horses), collected with care, will perhaps bring upon me the accusation of being a partisan of in-and-in breeding. In principle, I condemn its absolute use; but, within certain limits, I admit and advise it, especially in the commencement, when it becomes a question of founding and establishing a family designed to exercise a permanent influence upon the future improvement of a region.

Uniting together vices of conformation, character, and temperament, is rendering them indelible for ever. Uniting quality, beauty, and aptitude, it is preserving the monopoly of these in a single family.

Hence, I would like, when there appeared, on the turf or elsewhere, one of those envied types of which nature is generally so sparing, that judicious attempts, made with patience, should fix the qualities so apt to disappear, and collect, so to speak, all the sources whence they emanate.

The brothers, sisters, and collaterals, should be included, but once only, in these crossings, which might even go back, if it were still time, as far as the grandsires and dams, on account of the resemblance noticed between ancestors and their grandchildren.

Finally, the truly valuable and completely successful results of a family thus strengthened should be coupled according to the rules of intelligent crossing to the equally confirmed representatives of some other excellent family, fit to form new offspring.

CHAPTER IV.

OUGHT THE GRAY COLOR OF THE PERCHERON TO BE INFLEXIBLY MAINTAINED?

Formerly I liked the gray horse very much, and have more than once praised this color. But time has dissipated my illusions.

Thus, while acknowledging my former preferences for the gray horse over the horse of a different shade, I am now very far from showing myself exclusive, and quarreling with the mass of enlightened persons who seem desirous of adopting the dark colored coats. I only desire one thing, and that is to save the Percheron race, and to preserve to Perche its prosperity and its glory.

If I have liked the gray horse, it was from conviction, and not to court those who saw no safety outside the gray. But when the wisdom and the extreme intelligence of masters of science, prefering a less showy color, demonstrated to me that Perche might find an era of new glory and prosperity in changing the coat of its horse and thus enlarging the circle of consumption, I bowed meekly to their opinion. I liked the gray horse because I thought that Providence had created it gray in order that it might be able to withstand, during its work, the heat of the sun, and not be prostrated under its rays. I liked it gray, as the Arab likes his horse gray and his bournous of a whitish color; as the American planter likes his white cotton suit and his panama; as our soldier, in the field, liked, under the African or Mexican sky, the havelock which protected him against the rays of the burning luminary. I liked it gray because it seemed to me to recall more than any other the Arab, the primitive horse; because Perche having always possessed gray horses, I thought there was much more chance of finding, under this coat, the type of the country; because I had been rocked to sleep to the tune of that old ballad of our ancestors, celebrating Charles de Trie, the Percheron Seigneur, going forth to combat the English at the battle of Poitiers:

> " On charger white
> The sire of Trie
> Against the foe
> Has gone to war," etc. etc. ;

because, in a word, during my infancy, I had breathed the dust of the old manuscripts making mention of the white Percheron mares. I liked it gray, because, for the service of the post-coaches and couriers, in their long stages, in the middle of the night, the gray horse appeared to me more easy to guide than the horse of a dark color. Finally, it has always seemed to me that this coat was more becoming than any other the powerful form of a vigorous worker. Does not a good-looking, stalwart, and honest peasant please you better—is he not infinitely more at ease with the Gallic blouse covering his broad shoulders, than under the dark folds of a fashionable coat, which makes him appear awkward and abashed?

But everything is much changed. The country has no longer any special type in the midst of all this gray amalgamated with Brittany, Picardy, and Caux, of which the equine stock of Perche is now composed. If the Percheron should cease to be bound by this law of gray, if he should become of all shades, at the same time remaining good, and such as Perche knows how to make him, he would cease to be dishonored by those everlasting plagiarists, shamelessly calling themselves Percherons because they happen to be gray and have travelled across the Perche country. If he should become of all shades, in preserving the qualities and movement which are a feature of everything that the tonic grasses and the fine and vivifying air of Perche produces, he would not be reduced to the simple role of furnishing the 6,000 or 7,000 horses that the omnibuses and teamsters each year require, plus the 600 or 700 typical ones that foreign countries demand of Perche. He might, little by little, contribute to the satisfaction of the half-fancy and to the wants of the hunting and army equipages; he might advantageously replace the German horse, which we are obliged to employ in want of a better. Post-coaches no longer existing, there is no longer need of gray horses for the night in the midst of the darkness of the highways. Steam machinery, the indispensable substitute for the lack of human hands in the country, being destined to execute, in part, the labors of agriculture, the horse will be less employed there, and the one that will be called for, having fewer difficulties to overcome, can be lighter, more *distingué*, faster, and more fit for adaptation to the exigences of trade and fashion.—Finally, Fashion wishing, positively, no more gray horses, and the Percheron finding no longer a sufficient employment in the omnibuses, will soon find himself in a tight place if he do not take a fresh start, and make himself acceptable—if he do not conform to the exactions of the age, and become more stylish and darker colored.

It is settled, then, that he must put upon his back a less showy covering; but he can only do this on condition that he become, thanks to good crossings, more presentable and have a more stylish air. And, really, what is more ridiculous than a vulgar and common beast decked out with the livery of the fancy and private horse!

Let us occupy ourselves, then, seriously in looking up breeding stock of dark coats; the time to do this appears to me to have come. But where will we go to find them? Let us look about us and seek for this in Perche.

If you there find, under a dark coat, a fine Percheron, possessing all the qualities and specialties of the race, make haste, take him and color your horses. Sincerely, I give you this advice. Still, as in the present state of things, it is rare that the fine and the somber are met with together among the working races, by reason of the horror which has been professed, up to the present moment, for everything not gray, the best expedient would be to color the coat by means of fine, dark skin Arabs, or with good, well-chosen Norfolks, a subject that we will treat upon in the chapter of crossings. As to doing it otherwise, it is not to be thought of, the elements not existing in Perche.

This, however, is only a minor matter. The essential point is to unite the heavy to the *distingué*, weight to gait, mildness to vigor, hardiness to energetic temperament, steadiness and precocity; in a word, to repeat myself for the hundredth time, add a little more dash and style. Correct the defects of conformation, the imperfections of color, without weakening, without breaking up the harmony of the admirable qualities which have made of the Percheron the first horse of the age.

CHAPTER V.

PRESERVE PURE, AND WITHOUT INTERMIXTURE, THE THREE TYPES OF THE PERCHERON RACE—THE LIGHT HORSE, THE DRAFT HORSE, THE INTERMEDIATE HORSE.

We have spoken, in Chapter II, Part First, of the three types which the Percheron race presents—the light horse, the draft horse, and the intermediate or post horse. These three breeds come of the soil and are the product of ancient crosses. There is reason for their existing and for their marked peculiarities; and reason requires, then, that they should be preserved, and, in maintaining them always in their proper functions, we obey, in that progressive spirit which urges us to embellish everything. The first is destined to become the post horse and horse for private use, the surest and most agreeable means of locomotion. The second cannot be replaced for express carting, and for the builders and contractors of Paris and other large towns. To the third, the omnibuses always offer a steady market. Consequently, it is important to keep them without intermixture and to continue them uninterruptedly each in its respective class. Hence in seeking to add weight to a class it is necessary to avoid crossing it with a race superior in height, and different in conformation and temperament.

The heaviest and strongest of a class, united among themselves, will produce more surely the kind demanded than a too precipitate crossing. Nothing is more risky than crosses made without judgment. It is by them that harmony of form is destroyed, and a degenerate mongrel race is produced as the inevitable consequence. It is then important, in the reunion of types, never to lose sight of equality and similarity of conformation and qualities. But, at the same time, it is necessary to march with the age, study its tendencies, and be always ready to guide a movement which otherwise might drag you in its wake.

We must not lose sight of the fact that the services required of the Percheron horse are not the same as formerly. The omnibus service, especially, which, scarcely ten years ago, was considered the mildest, has, at present, become the hardest, and the one which requires heavy horses, uniting speed with strength.

On the other hand, as a consequence of the great changes in the life and means of conveyance of the wealthy, the Percheron race has been most prominently brought forward. Almost all ranks of the upper classes have now adopted the Percheron horse of the light kind for their private uses, hunts and drives in the country. The fondness for rapid traveling rendering these classes more exacting than formerly, the necessity has arisen of finding in Perche, specimens with weight and speed with a light and stylish form. Accordingly, it becomes necessary to find means of adding the greatest possible speed to the other valuable characteristics of the Percheron horse. To reach this result promptly, we should have recourse to the Arabian stallion, and this, surely, would be the quickest means. But as I do not find this Percheron race, in its present state, sufficiently prepared for this alliance, and as I think that it still needs two or three generations of preparatory crossings with itself, it will be necessary to commence, in order to attain this end, by close interbreeding.

We should, at first, commence by exploring the Percheron centers devoted exclusively to the rearing of mares, and, in these places, we should particularly visit the localities in which they have no great development as to height. Here we would select a group of from fifteen to twenty fillies, the best, the finest limbed, the most compact, the fastest trotters, and having for an extreme maximum the height of 15'|, to 16 hands.

The same course should be pursued in the regions where the colts are raised, and there choice should be made of some light stallions, approaching, as much as possible, to the mares in form and qualities.

All the best foals, then, should be in their turn subjected to couplings conducted with the same care, and among the third generation would be found types sufficiently confirmed, either as founders of a race among themselves, or for crossing with the Arab, of which we will speak in the following chapter.

If a little larger size be required, it would not be necessary to have recourse to other types than those which I have just indicated. Well-balanced horses favor every modification. More tonic, substantial nourishment, and more fertile meadows would increase the height and weight, as well as the strength and spirit.

Do you desire omnibus horses?—You can obtain them by selecting in the regions which best produce the post-horse, the strongest types, the heaviest bodied, the most favored as to height, and the fastest trotters. But never yield any of these three points: weight, spirit, and speed.

The animals the nearest alike in size and form should then be coupled together, after the manner indicated above, and when weight, spirit, and speed, are found without failing in all the progeny, it will then be time, but not till then, to add style. The Arabian stallion, whose tendency, as we will see later, is to produce heavier and stronger than himself, while at the same time imparting his mark of supreme distinction, might then be introduced to embellish and confirm our good results.

The heavy draft and the express wagon horses should have weight: this is a *sine qua non* condition; but it would be a great mistake to confine ourselves exclusively to mere size. They should possess powerful limbs and muscles, joined to great spirit. This crossing, although the easiest, would also present great dangers should we be satisfied with weight alone; we would soon arrive at the mere lymphatic horse. It is, therefore, urgent, for the breeds possessing requisite strength, to choose those which are the most *distingué*, the most nervous, the finest limbed, and the most spirited, and to avoid the sluggish and lymphatic. These will be found in the elevated and dry centers, where the food is plenty and nutritious.

If Perche proper, Beauce, and the environs of Châteaudun, should not be capable of furnishing their complete contingent in this specialty (as I believe they cannot,) some good specimens could be met with among the Percheron colts raised in the environs of Bernay and on the plains of Sens.

This variety (the draft-horse) demands a great deal less care in the choice of the dams and sires. It is infinitely more elementary, since weight is principally sought after. Still, it is well, even indispensable, to select individuals short coupled and with good quarters, to hold out under the enormous loads they are obliged to draw. The means resorted to to accomplish this are judicious crosses, constantly made with a well-determined and always identical idea, tending to increase weight and strength, while preserving spirit and vigor, abundant nourishment, and breeding in those sections naturally most propitious to style and size. Soon, Perche, placed in a situation without a rival for the present, and, above all, for the future, might forever avoid asking any thing of foreign crossings. For though the choice of the stallion and the mare is so important in the *production* of the foal, the climate, the kind of food, the agricultural habits, and, finally, the adaptation of the region to horse breeding, are of a great deal more importance in the *development* of the animal. It becomes, then, somewhat difficult to indicate accurately to what types, in such particular cases, the preference should be awarded. The best are those which most nearly meet the wants of the section.

CHAPTER VI.

IMPROVEMENT OF THE BREED BY MEANS OF FOREIGN CROSSINGS.

However, if with strength acquired and faults corrected, style is not attained, it may be sought after by judicious crosses with well-chosen foreign types.

Two different breeds present themselves to us as means of improving our stock by the introduction of foreign blood: the Arabian, and the English, with its variations. Starting from this point, let us study both and endeavor to discover, by analogy, which one would best suit, or, rather, which one is the least unfavorable to the purpose.

I will examine, one after another, these two methods in detail, leaving to the cultivator, who is most interested in the question, the choice of employing that which seems to him the best and the most appropriate, taking into view the fertility and the nature of his section. But I must, from the beginning, lay down as a principle that both are more expensive than is interbreeding. A race to become fit to receive a foreign cross, should be prepared for it in advance, in order to shorten, as much as possible, the distance existing between the breed so formed and proved and that which we seek to create.

In fact, the foreign cross can do no good, unless the desired qualities in the race upon which it is made are permanent, fixed, and characteristic.

Why not think also of increasing our resources by better cultivation, by liberal feeding, by choosing, as I have said above, among the race of the country, the most perfect types and those most likely to correct what is vicious while they impart their own good qualities? Methods of this kind, pursued for a long time and persistently, are alone capable of preparing, without inconvenience, for a foreign cross.

Drain your wet meadows, irrigate your hill-sides, fertilize your soil by the use of improving manures, make productive fields everywhere, create meadows, grow heavy oats, enlarge your stables and make them clean, healthy and airy. When you have done this, then, but not before, you can cross your races with foreign blood, more delicate than yours and accustomed to and requiring greater care and attention.

I know that this slowly progressive manner does not possess the sympathies of those who, at the commencement, are restless at not having already reached the goal. But it is sure and free from errors, whilst the other, (France has but too many examples of this), after money squandered and years wasted, reduces the breeder who has recourse to it to a more miserable condition than that from which he wished to escape.

Our *furia francese*, which renders us irresistible in war, our fancy for new fashions, which gives birth to those wonders which the world hails with ecstacy, and

3

our proverbial inconstancy, cause us almost always to go astray in breeding. Fashion has no sooner praised horses of such and such a race, of this or that model, or such and such a coat, than we must immediately produce the like, without first ascertaining whether or no our race be prepared for crossing with them. The result of such crosses would be about as valuable as a discussion between a fishwoman and an academician!

Nature, left to herself, is a thousand times more intelligent than the man of systems. Are there ever found, among the wild animals, among lions, tigers, stags, chamois, etc., either spavins, tumors, periodical inflammations, or any of those thousand infirmities with which our domestic horse is afflicted?—And here is the reason: in the rutting season, the possession of the females becomes the incitement to bloody battles. It is always the strongest, the most vigorous, the bravest, the most venturesome, and the best made stallion, which receives as a reward for his victory, the submission and the admiring love of the harem.

But I assume Perche prepared, by numerous and good crossings of the race within itself, to try, with more sureness, foreign crossings. Two principal types, as we have just seen, are presented for this: the Arab type and the English, which is itself derived from the Arab.

The foreign cross I only speak of with diffidence, because with it I enter unknown regions of inductions and perhaps, alas! into ways of deception and ruin, if it is not effected with the greatest prudence and judgment.

Foreign crossings, systematically effected from the north to the south, and from the south to the north, have had Buffon for their apostle, and, under the cloak of his genius, and thanks to the authority of his word, they have reached everywhere. But how enumerate the evils brought about by a school, whose disciples are still numerous, thanks to a perseverance irritated but not deterred by failure ? These evils have been branded in large characters on all our breeds, since that day when they became the objects, not of constant and uniform care, but considered as subjects of no consequence, upon which individuals might experiment in order to test their theories, and set themselves up as teachers.

Since then, we have no more types properly belonging to distinct districts, but a confused assembly, combining with rare qualities the defects of this or that cross and twenty others more. Everywhere in turn, from one region or another, were stallions employed of different types and races: those of the south transported to the north, and those of the north to the south; and that without preparation, and without attention to the differences of soil and climate of the various regions. All these practices have injured our breeds without successfully retaining their own native qualities.

CHAPTER VII.

THE ARAB CROSSING.

I commence with the Arab crossing. Two motives have induced me to follow this classification:

1st. The Arabian is the type horse, and the type should be examined before its derivatives.

2nd. The Percheron shows a very great analogy, by his coat, conformation, character of race, mild disposition, and endurance, to the Arab, of which he seems to be the son, notwithstanding certain differences, the result of time, climate, and the region in which he is bred and in which he lives.

I have said that the Percheron horse exhibits in common with the Arab numerous marks of a common parentage and relationship: these marks are very obvious. A Percheron, a true Percheron, for some still exist, (as the famous *Toulouse* of M. Chéradame, of Ecouché; and the renowned *Jean-le-Blanc* of M. Miard, of Villers, near Sap, in the department of the Orne, etc., etc.,) placed alongside of an Arab, presents, notwithstanding his heavier and grosser form, analogies with him so striking that we are easily induced to believe them undoubted relations.

The Percheron of the primitive type has a gray coat like the Arab; and like him an abundant and silky mane, a fine skin, and a large, prominent, and expressive eye; a broad forehead, dilated nostrils, and a full and deep chest, although, the girth, with him, as with the Arab, is always lacking in fullness; more bony and leaner limbs, and less covered with hair than those of other draft-horse families.

He has not, it is true, the fine haunch and fine form of the shoulder, nor that swan-like neck which distinguishes the Arab; but it must not be forgotten that for ages he has been employed for draft purposes, and these habits have imparted to his bony frame an anatomical structure, a combination of levers adapted to the work he is called upon to perform. He has not, I again acknowledge, such a fine skin as the Arab, nor his prettily rounded, oval, and small foot; but we must remember the fact that he lives under a cold climate, upon elevated plains, where nature gives him for a covering a thicker skin and a warmer coat, and that he has been for ages stepping upon a moist, clayey soil.

In all that remains in him, we recognize a heavy Arab, modified and remodeled by climate and peculiar circumstances. He has remained mild and laborious, like his sire; he is brought up, like him, in the midst of the family, and, like him, he possesses in a very high degree the faculty of easy acclimation. He acquires this in the midst of the numerous migrations he accomplishes in Perche, the counterpart of those that the type horse makes upon the sands of the desert. A final comparison, which has not, as yet, been sufficiently noticed, is, that, like the Arab, he has no need of being mutilated in order to be trained, managed and kept without danger. In a word, the Percheròn, notwithstanding the ages which separate them, presents an affinity as close as possible with the primitive horse, which is the Arab.

From this similarity of form and probable relationship, comes the thought of new alliances. But in order to form a more easy estimate of their effects, it will not be without interest to classify the horses with reference to their origin. This classification produces three very distinct groups: the primitive horse, the natural horse, and the compound horse.

The *Primitive Horse*, oriental in its origin, is the pure Arabian horse; no other is acknowledged.

During the time of the crusaders, as we have already said in our first part, in consequence of wars and all kinds of excursions, individuals of this race were spread over almost all parts of the globe. Although at first the prestige which their superior merits deserved led to their being bred in-and-in, these exiles were placed under different latitudes, in different atmospheric and hygienic conditions, which gradually modified their qualities and led to the degeneracy of the race. And it became more or less degenerate in proportion as the soil upon which the colts were foaled was colder, poorer, and more inhospitable; *for the horse is as much, and more, the son of the soil upon which he is foaled and reared as he is of his sire and dam.*

This fact has no need of proof. We see it every day before our eyes in studying at home the changes that our French breeds themselves undergo when transported from one province to another. It might, however, be thought that these new latitudes, these new regions, would differ but little from those in which they lived.

The first change that the primitive horse undergoes, from the difference of the regions into which he has been transplanted, being due to nature itself, we call the result the *Natural Horse.*—Here it is proper to remark how wise nature always is. If it modify the primitive horse for the worse, it modifies him, however, under conditions better adapted to his wants. In rendering him more puny, it renders him more temperate, and enables him to live and to nourish himself upon the food that the locality is able to furnish. Submitted to the trials and the fatigues of war, and to all the miseries in its train, the natural horse, badly built, ungainly and puny as he is, endures fatigue almost as well as the primitive horse.

The *Cross-bred Horse* is, as his name indicates, the issue of a sire and dam 'of different breeds. This crossing, made with a view to improvement, may give, when judicious, more elegant, better made, and finer-bodied progeny and also quicker in their various gaits, but always requiring, especially if derived from the English, exceptional care, and so much the more particular as they are of a more *distingué* nature.

Abandoned to himself, deprived of blankets, shelter, grooming, and oats, the cross-bred deteriorates early, and in war perishes miserably, while the natural and the primitive horse thrives in browsing upon the scantiest herbage. On this score, our two campaigns of the Crimea and Italy have furnished unquestionable proofs.

Such is the result chiefly obtained with the too *distingué* English horse, even when delivered to the best working mares. In the army, especially, is this point settled; they have there recognized and proved that the worst subjects were always the issue of authors having too much blood and too impressionable. No horses are more apt than these to provoke and render ill humored, and, if I may so speak, ruin the temper of the men placed over them.

When a working race is crossed with the English, it is indispensable that the stallion should be well bred and be but a quarter blood,—a quarter at the utmost. And the manner of balancing the blood is neither an indifferent thing nor a thing to be neglected. We should be very careful not to accept as such the product of a full-blooded or even half-blooded stallion and a common mare, but should rather take the product, ameliorated through generations, of strong races that have been gradually perfected, such as, for instance, certain Norfolk horses, certain roadsters and trotters, of which old *Jaggard* was a type, and of which *Performer*, although not so marked, vaguely recalled the memory.

Since I have mentioned the name of Norfolk, let me say, that after the Arab race, of all the foreign ones, the Norfolk trotter is the one which seems to me to offer the greatest advantages in an alliance with the Percheron. With both, good qualities and defects are diverse, so that they can complete and correct each other by means of a wisely combined and carefully studied connection.

The Norfolk horse has, it is true, an ugly head, and his eye is small and destitute of expression; but his neck, with good lines, starts well from his breast; his shoulder is fine and well-sloped; his chest magnificent, and his girth enormous; his loins broad, well-sustained and well-attached; his haunches long, his croup horizontal; his buttocks well filled out and low; and his limbs strong, but not quite free enough from fat; nor is his action always sufficiently stylish, yet he has a quick and free gait.

Give to this horse a mare having a fine and expressive head, lighted up with a large, intelligent, well-opened eye; let her possess lean, elegant, and perfect limbs, and, a hundred to one, you will get a valuable colt. But, with the Norfolk, as with all others, there are degrees, and

if I cross the Channel in search of a stock horse, I should
wish him to possess the following qualities:

This stallion should be rather large, have thick and
strong limbs, chest fully developed, the girth as great as
possible, very heavy in the hind-quarters, buttocks descending well, forehead broad and open, and the eye large and
expressive. He should be always shorter in height than
the mares, but quite as broad, and, I repeat it, as short-
limbed as possible, on account of an invariable, innate tendency of the English horse to height and thinness. He
should be neither cross, nor, above all, affected with that
nervous sensitiveness too common in the English breeds.
His action should be quick, well kept up, bold and square.
He should have, if possible, a decided and well-pronounced
color, either a dark bay or a chestnut. Breeding stock
of his get should be chosen under identical conditions,
and then they would be on a footing with him, although,
logically speaking, there would be always an inclination
to prefer the type to the sub-type.

But, at present, it is easy to be deceived, even in England, in regard to the stock of the country. There is less
risk in using, if he can be found, a good, heavy Anglo-
Norman horse, bred and reared under our eyes in Merlerault or on the plains of Alençon, than a spurious English
one, which is often none other than a forlorn hope of some
nameless region. In fact, from certain appearances, there
is reason to fear that persons from the other side of the
Channel visit the continent to do a smart thing, and purchase heavy, lymphatic colts to bring up on some English
farm, and then resell them as Norfolk horses. What kind
of improvement is to be expected from such means?
We should always respect the will of nature, which allows
us to assist her in her course, but we should never violate
her laws.

Man vainly wishes to force nature with all these crosses, at which she takes exceptions. To all this so-called

science she opposes her relentless logic; these products are an unnatural brood, which she refuses to acknowledge as her own. She stops short, and, no matter how good these results may appear in themselves, the error crops out, and it is known by experience that they almost all fail when put to the test of breeding.

But suppose every measure of prudence taken, even suppose there has been no mistake, most of the produce resulting from this first crossing will be, generally, lighter built than their dams. However, among the number there will be found some which, uniting weight to beauty, will constitute good types with athletic and regular forms. The latter only should be preserved, and these only can be usefully employed, either among themselves or outside of their own families, in the improvement of our stock.

At the second crossing, the imperfections observed at the first will disappear in a great measure, and from the third crossing, with constant care, unflinching attention, and unwearied patience, the difficult problem will be solved: size combined with vigor, hardiness of constitution with style, and weight with elegance.

If, on the contary, by wishing to make too quick progress, there should be too much difference between the stallion and the mare, the resulting stock, although in appearance successful, will always prove bad breeders, giving ungainly results, with blemishes which would never have occurred in proceeding wisely, especially not in improving by means of *the primitive horse*, all of whose ancestors are of the same race.

This latter crossing, that is, with the Arab, may sometimes give slower, but with it we are always sure to obtain finally better results. Thus in making choice of the best Percheron mares and crossing them with fine, but the stoutest possible, Arabs, we would advance towards certain improvements, and at the end of a few generations, we would be sure to find at each foaling season fine types,

3*

combining with the strength and docility of the dams the style, spirit, and intelligence, of the sires. For, it must not be forgotten, work requires intelligent horses; the more they are gifted with this quality, the longer they last and the more useful their services.

If the drunken driver of the Lyons Railroad, whose adventure is known the world over, had not had for his working companion a brute as nobly intelligent as the old horse *Lapin*, employed in hauling dirt carts, he would surely have perished. The driver having fallen in a state of intoxication on the railroad, before a train descending a grade, was on the point of being run over, when the horse, seeing him in this perilous situation and at the risk of being himself crushed, seized him by the waist and lifted him off the track. This deed, performed under the eyes of several squads of workmen, was soon known over the whole line, and won for *Lapin* the title of *The (invalid's and workingmen's) Adopted Son*, a nobly gained title and well-merited reward, if ever there was one.

In the legends of all times are to be found examples of the intelligence of the oriental horse; but I have never heard quoted a single one in regard to the English thoroughbred, which seems only formed for pride, gluttony, and brutality. As an example of the sagacity of the Arab, I will limit myself to mentioning a fact witnessed by all the officers of the school of Saumur. At this school there was an old Arabian known to the whole army. One day, a lady having her handkerchief scented with, I know not what perfume, passed in front of the veteran, caressing and feeding him with dainties. From that time on, the officer who accompanied the lady could never enter her parlor, although the odor of the perfume was imperceptible to all, but the horse, on his return, was aware of the fact, and bore witness to it, each time, by neighing and by a hundred expressions of pleasure.

The vigor and pluck of the oriental horse have passed

into a proverb. There is not a soldier in our army who cannot bear testimony to this.

The horses of the English cavalry almost all perished in the Crimean war, whilst our Algerian horses almost all returned. In the Italian war our Algerian horses bore well the fatigues of the campaign, where the horses springing from the English were decimated.

It appears impossible that these two proofs should have no signification and should not teach a lesson. Ought it not to be concluded from them that the war-horse, that is the horse for endurance, should only be of Arab blood or at least derived from the Arab?

And are we not justified in believing that what has taken place with the war-horse applies also to other horses destined for continuous work? Hence are we not right in always preferring the Arab to the English stallion, when it is a question of improving the different breeds of work and draft-horses, as well as the war horse?

The Arabian stallion would seem so much the more fit for this use, as a long experience has proved that his get upon our native mares are much heavier than himself; they, at the same time, always transmitting a rich, unblemished blood and a solid frame—qualities which are preserved indefinitely.

The Arab horse imparts, also, great endurance to his progeny, and without going back as far as the turf, where we see figuring on the top round of the ladder *Arlequin, Zephyr, Valencia, Corysandre* the Lorraine, whose dam was an Arabian of *Deux-Ponts, Anthony, Eylau, Kasbas,* and *Palmyre,* let us be satisfied with citing in mass, all the fine and spirited breeds of Limousin, Navarre, Bigorre, Tarbes, and Auvergne, showing in every pore the presence of the Oriental blood.

It is also especially to be remarked, although the Arab does not trot and only gallops, that all his get are quick, square trotters. We can produce numberless examples

of this, although Arab blood has been infinitely less dis-
seminated than any other in our Northern districts.

We can cite the famous *Eclipse* of M. de Narbonne,
the no less famous *Herminie* of M. Forcinal, all the descendants of *Bacha, Aslan* and *Gallipoli*, which were
matchless, and the noble sons of *Massoud, Eylau,* and
Noteur. But, as all these have a certain amount of English blood joined to the Arab, we shall be answered:—It
was the English blood that trotted and gave them their
winning points.—We will confine ourselves to citing only
the sons of *Bédouin*, all admirable trotters, though all
coming of poor Brittany mares, the *Kerims*, the *Avisos*,
and the *Moggys*, whose fine action invariably attracts the
attention of every one.

But the endurance possessed by the Arab in so eminent a
degree is not the only quality to be considered. It is also
the opinion of the best breeders that the race is good tempered, docile, patient, of great precocity, and easily raised,
all of which qualities it invariably transmits to its get.

No steeple-chase horses have shown themselves more
intelligent than *Pledge, Raphael, Senora*, and above all
the immortal *Franc-Picard*, by whom the best riders
found themselves excelled in the art of measuring an ob-
stacle and mastering it skillfully ; also, these were deep in
the Arab blood. If *Auricula*, notwithstanding he was a
son of *Baron*, with his variable and peevish temper has
shown himself to be, when he chose, one of the best leap-
ers of our age, it is because through his dam he is of Arab
blood.

From all these considerations the Arabian seems greatly
preferable to the English horse, which exacts, moreover,
too much tact and skill on the part of man. The education of the wagon driver is not yet sufficiently advanced
for him to be able to reap all the advantages claimed of
the working races. The irritability of the English horse,
his impatience, and his nervousness, which are, doubtless,

of utility on the turf, are transmitted to all his descendants, which for this very reason are less fit for work, less governable, and more trying to the patience of the raw and ignorant driver during protracted service.

All who have raised colts out of common mares by Arabians are unanimous in opinion, and we have ourselves proved it, that their get is generally even tempered, of a mild, willing, and quiet disposition, easily and cheaply reared, and fit for work at three years old, thus paying for their keep.

It is quite the contrary with the colt of English blood. He, by reason of his fractiousness, his nervous ardor, his exacting nature, and his slow growth, requires a degree of care and management which does not permit him to render any essential service before the age of five years.

It results from this that the Arabian progeny, even at the first crossing, which is always the most difficult and critical, pays for its nourishment from the age of three years, whilst the English does not pay until he has reached five years, and this without counting the greater expense of his raising and the difficulty of finding men capable of breaking and training him without accident and bringing him safe to that quinquennial period.

Were their qualities the same, the Arabian would cost much less to the breeder than the English horse. To the former, then, should always be given the preference in moderately rich countries where agriculture has not arrived at great perfection. Thus it was by means of the Arabian that Limousin, Navarre, Bigorre, the plains of Tarbes and Auvergne, all countries neither very fertile nor wealthy, have formed their unrivalled horses, the hardiness of which suited the productions of the soil. These being unsuited to the more delicate and less vigorous English horse, its introduction was an injury to the native stock. In our days, Limousin has been ruined by the introduction of English blood, as formerly, in the district of Tarbes, three important breeders, Messrs. de Gontaut, de Bouillac, and de Montréal, ruined their studs with the English cross.

The Arabian can be used without fear upon the undulating slopes of elevated hills, and upon thin stony lands where agriculture is but little advanced; but the English horse requires rich, well-cultivated meadows and grassy valleys.

As regards form, the Arab cross is the surest. The sire being, if I may so speak, *sui generis*, of a confirmed race, and possessing for ages a like shape, his get always resemble him, no matter what may be the race, color, shape, and derivation, of the dam. Only, in consequence of the warmth and strength of his blood, the progeny is always larger and heavier than the sire.

It is not so with the English horse. Made up, and not having the same confirmed nature as the Arab, he has not the same sureness in generating. Sometimes his get is large and sometimes small. His progeny may be spare or may be stout. This comes from his ancestors being at times of one height and at times of another, and often resembling different types.

We have dwelt, perhaps, at too great length upon our preference for the Arab cross; it now remains to put it in practice. The method to be pursued in making this cross is simple.

Having an Arabian of pure race, the heaviest and finest bodied that can be found, put him to the heaviest and strongest short-limbed mares. Sell the male produce of this cross, unless it has been a perfect success. Be less strict with the fillies, reject a smaller number, and use the good for breeding. As much as their conformation will permit, and in order to fix the Arab blood in a deeper and more indelible manner, some choice specimens may be put either to their sire himself, or to such of the half-brothers as should have proved themselves the best. But beyond the first trial,

consanguineous crossings should never again be contracted, except under exceedingly rare circumstances, or under
great temptation. The dam of one of the most justly
celebrated horses of our times is the result of breeding
a stallion to his dam. From and after the second
generation, colts and fillies, provided their merit had ren-
dered them worthy of being used as producers, might be
taken as types, and as a starting point of a solid and sure
improvement of the race of a country.

When, in consequence of age and numerous generations
of his own get growing up around him, the common sire
might be exposed to alliances with his grand-children, it
would become indispensable to transfer him to a distant
district by proceeding in the manner indicated above.

After such an infusion of warm blood many years might
elapse without the necessity of recurring again to Arabian
stock. But if it should be remarked that its distinctive
characteristics commenced to disappear from the breed,
and the action became less free and light, it should be
again resorted to immediately, following the same method
as before.

The light draft types at first obtained, might, according
to the districts in which they are raised, be transformed
into the posting, omnibus, and even heavy draft types.
But all should be done with time and without haste nor even
wishing to depart from a wise and prudent moderation.

I cannot terminate this chapter without warning the
breeder against a peculiarity which hardly ever fails to strike
a person, who, for the first time, makes a trial of the Arab
cross, and which has even induced some to abandon this
method without reaping its fruits. I desire to speak of a
certain disproportion, more apparent than real, of the limbs
with the body. It is thus explained: The Arabian, born
and raised in a poor and barren country, is no sooner
transported to a more fertile region, than a certain fullness
of the body is an immediate consequence of this change.

His progeny, easily fattened, rapidly become corpulent. It results from this, that although strongly limbed, they appear, for a large body, to have but weak extremities. But have patience ; oats will draw in and strengthen those inflated flanks, and, after the second generation, the stomach of the colt will enlarge on account of the food being more abundant than concentrated, the fat will disappear, and his compact and solid limbs will appear what they really are.

CHAPTER VIII.

THE ENGLISH CROSS.

English blood, infused with judgment, allies well with the Percheron race, and we have met with perfectly successful results in the midst of the disappointments which have been the consequences of injudicious crossing. Too often these crossings have been effected in violation of common sense, without any attention to the distance which separates the blood horse from the common, low-bred Percheron mare, she having no affinity with him. But these trials require science, wealth, and perseverance, and are far from being within the reach of ordinary breeders. Those who would succeed must possess the talent of waiting, for unfortunately the rearing of the resulting progeny is a burden. Their slow development renders them but little fit for the labors to which the farmer is in the habit of consigning his colts. Then, they cannot, like the young Percheron, pass from hand to hand, and thus they find themselves stripped of the only advantage which renders the raising of the draft colts so profitable : avoiding embarrassment and affording a prompt profit to

PRINCE IMPERIAL.—FRENCH NORMAN.

all through whose hands they pass. In fact, it can easily be conceived how favorably, at present, are these chances of profit distributed among several hands. The capital invested is soon returned; and thus this operation is within the reach of all purses.

The issue of English blood, if judiciously managed, will some day be finer than the unimproved Percheron. But, although carefully looked after and abundantly fed, he will remain puny during his early growth, and therefore his account can only be closed at a distant date. By whom, then, is he to be raised? By the farmer rich in ready money? In every country such men are rare. By the large landed proprietor? But he is not a breeder, or if he be, it is only of race-horses.

Some half-blood English stallions noted for strength and weight, standing at Mesle-sur-Sarthe, Courtomer, and Nogent-le-Rotrou, have produced fine coach and draft-horses, but their number has always been rather limited, and they have nearly all been raised without care, like the half-blood colt simply at pasture; consequently, the profit accruing has been nothing, or nearly nothing, and these have been able to add nothing useful in the way of example and imitation.

On the contrary, in Lower Perche, commencing at Nogent and extending as far as Vendôme, the draft-horse, properly speaking, is the only one that has been raised. The wagon-horse is there only met with as an exception, and the cultivator is far from being the worse off on this account. Witness the prosperity of Montdoubleau, which has become the first market of Europe; witness the splendid and spirited trotting mares it produces every year, and of which the *Julies* of M. Derré and the *Sarahs* of M. Lamoureux are glorious specimens.

Perche has seen but twice, to our knowledge, good and irrefutable results obtained from the English crossing with her race—the first, with *Sandy;* the second, with *Bay-*

ard. Sandy was a draft stallion, with a long and silky
mane, a perfectly white coat, and with a high and grace-
ful gait like that of an oriental horse; lean and strong
legs, a short head, dilated nostrils, and a large and intelligent eye. Although foaled in England, this horse was ev-
idently not English ; he must have come of eastern blood,
as this is so often seen among our neighbors who successfully use the Arab blood in the formation of their draft
and hunting races.

As for *Bayard*, he was a son of a Percheron mare belonging to M. Viel, of Chiffreville, near Argenton, one
of the finest and purest ever seen. This mare had been
bred to *Idalis*, a small and well-knit wagon-horse, son
of *Don Quichotte*, who descended from the thoroughbred
brood-mare *Moina*. Consequently, *Bayard* had in his
veins some of the best oriental blood, and it is to this circumstance that is attributed the vigor, gait, and beauty,
of all his progeny.

Perhaps the two stallions *Benvenuto* and *Fandango*,
which passed for Anglo-Percherons, and which have been
cited as types of draft-horse stallions, will be held up to
me as a refutation. *Benvenuto*, the stallion from Pin,
which has produced well in Perche, was not the son of
Eastham and a Percheron mare, as was said at the time
in order to have him accepted by the government, but was
really out of a Percheron mare by a Percheron stallion
coming from the neighborhood of Bellesme, and the de-
scendant of Arabian stallions which had been standing in
that district.

Fandango, the other crossed Percheron, uniformly a
successful stallion, had double cross, on the sire's side, of
the blood of the Arabian *Dagout*, and his dam, whose
pedigree has also been explained to me, came likewise
from near *Bellesme*.

A Percheron stallion called *Jean-le-Blanc*, native of
Mauves, and sold about the year 1825 to a M. Viard of

Villers, in Ouche, near Sap, (department of the Orne,) has been the sole improving agent of the equine race in Ouche, which, up to that time, was reduced to miserable small horses without any stamp or value. Although heavy, powerful, and, indeed, a shaft-horse, his gait and an indescribable something pervading his whole body, recalled so thoroughly the idea of the oriental family that one was disposed to take him for an enlarged Arabian. This fact, often related to us, excited our curiosity. We did not rest until pressing inquiry upon inquiry, one after another, we ascertained that his family had been crossed with a stallion from the Pin stables, standing at the Chateau of Côèsmes, near Bellesme. And, what was this stallion? The Arab *Gallipoli!*

What can be inferred from these facts, if it be not that the crossings which have best succeeded in Perche have been those of the Arab, and that the English crosses have only succeeded when tempered by contact with the Arab?

But if the absolute want of stallions for improving the breed be felt among the pure Percherons; if it be impossible to procure either good Arabs or heavy English, freshly tempered with Arab blood; if important and powerful considerations compel a recourse to the English cross, the latter should only be accepted intelligently and under good and wise conditions. Therefore we ask leave to refer the reader particularly to what we have already advanced in the preceding chapter upon the choice of an English stallion.

In Brittany, in the department of Finisterre, we have often heard it declared by quite a large number of breeders, that for having wished to proceed too fast in that way, they had, from the commencement, experienced numberless disappointments, the second generation from the English cross being always inferior to the first. From stout sires and dams, who, from their general appearance might be classed in the category of heavy-draft, there daily came ungainly stock, thin, lanky, leggy, and without weight in the hind-quarter, unattractive, of a difficult sale when young, and proving a veritable misfortune to the small farmer counting upon the sale of the colt to pay his rent and having neither the place nor means to raise him. This stock was, moreover, the object of another disappointment quite as serious as the first; rarely was a good worker to be found among this burdensome race.

Is not this tall, lank, weak,—in a word this abortive progeny,—issue of strong and hardy parents, a strange and discouraging result? "Oh! why is this?" exclaimed the Brittany cultivators. There was a simple reason for it, of which they had not learned the value. They proceeded with race-horse speed in the way of crossing, and gave no oats. They were ignorant of the requirements of the *distingué* horse; they did not know that in the sire and dam, or at least in one of them, there was circulating more or less English blood, which produces strange results in proportion as it leaves its native place and reaches a poor country or one of hard work, and in which it no longer receives the prodigal care of its native land.

We have said that the Arab preserves indefinitely his warm blood and constantly gives what he has not even himself,—although this truth resembles a paradox,—that is: a powerful appearance and a strong frame. It is not the same with the English horse and his derivatives; they become thin and always degenerate. If their progeny be not fed with oats without stint,—they require this, and are heavy eaters, like everything which comes from the north, —their blood grows poorer rapidly. In successive generations of these families, born in a dull and damp atmosphere scarcely ever visited by the sun, the legs become lean and lanky. It is necessary to recur incessantly to new drafts of English upon English, always expensive and requiring additional care, without taking into account that the result of too great an infusion of this peevish and

often irascible blood would be to destroy the heavy-draft
race—a race that I would like to see preserved intact
alongside of the two others, though he be not quite
suited to a country as hilly as Perche. He might, doubtless, plow successfully the vast and smooth plains of
Beauce; but this is not the lot of all. I look for him in
that busy country called Perche, where he must, without
rest or pity, with a shoulder free from all tenderness, drag
heavy vehicles to the tops of hills, and it will please me
to see the play of his haunches and limbs in descending
with these loads bravely and without flinching to the bottom of the valleys.

Do you expect, also, from a horse derived from English
blood that cool, restrained, and ever fresh energy, that
courageous patience of which the Percheron, every day,
gives an example in the omnibuses of the streets of Paris?
Dragging at a trot heavy loads, the weight of which
frightens the imagination; stopping short, both in ascend-
ing or descending; starting off freely and always without
balking; never sulking at his work or food, and fearing
neither heat nor cold: this is a specimen of Percheron
qualities.

Do you expect from an unjudicious cross with English
blood a good, heavy draft-horse, a good shaft-horse, or
a true wagon-horse? No one has now any illusion on
this score.

In London, a traction of only about 2,000 lbs. is required of a draft-horse. In Paris, the horses harnessed to the
heavy stone carts are required to drag as much as 5,000
lbs. each, and often even more.

What will dealers in heavy draft-horses do? The trade
is already taxed to supply the demand. For long
experience has taught, and unjudicious crosses have
proved the English horse and his derivatives to be unfit
for this purpose, for they are too nervous and not sufficiently staunch. Thus, the trade avoids them by instinct,

and by instinct avoids every thing resembling them. And, on the other hand, it seizes hold of and clings eagerly to every indication that can serve it as a sign or mark— every thing that can guide it in the search for what it likes, and every thing that can guard against its opposite.

Hence, it repels and proscribes the dark-colored coats without examination and reflection, because they are considered the colors of the English horse; it accepts the grays with confidence, because with them it perceives the absence of the dreaded blood, and in them it has found that which satisfies all its wants. Would we have arrived at this point if we had been prudent, and had the cross-breeding been better understood?

Finally, what is there at the end of this negative pole and this positive pole? There is the Percheron on whom has devolved, and will devolve for a long time yet, the rude and killing mission of executing the feats of strength exacted of him by modern civilization. The profits in supplying the demand, accrue, and will accrue for a long time to the producer.

Thus so long as machinery does not replace the horse in the traction of heavy carriages, so long as the necessity for hard labor remains, requiring strength, intelligence, endurance, and willingness, so long to the Percheron alone will be reserved the dangerous honor of being the great draft power, and the price of this matchless agent will increase in proportion to the growing impossibility of finding his substitute.

It is now the time, while crossing the active and trotting breeds with the Arab or with the well-chosen English horse, to carefully preserve the heavy draft-horse, and, by means of persevering and judicious crossing, retain for him his marked superiority.

These crossings, which I will sum up in concluding, may find a powerful aid in the creation of a Stud-book of the Percheron breed.

CHAPTER IX.

IMPROVEMENT BY MEANS OF THE STUD-BOOK.

The Percheron breed is old enough, is propagated with sufficient uniformity, and presents sufficiently marked typical qualities to authorize us in claiming, in favor of its members, the characteristics and the title of a separate and distinct breed. Consequently, a Stud-book, recording its pedigrees, would not be out of place. This book would have the effect of concentrating the efforts of all the breeders, giving them a definite direction, and at the same time it would designate stallions foreign to the race, and which, up to the present time, have been presented with impunity as Percherons.

England exhibits a curious example of the influence of the Stud-book in the improvement of a breed. The equine and bovine races of that country, before the establishment of the Stud and Herd-books, were but rudimental.

The small number of colts of the Royal mares by Eastern stallions would have been lost had they not been classed together in families in a special book.

The discovery of the value of the bull *Hubback* would have been to no purpose had his descendants not been classified by themselves in an authentic manner.

For it is especially, and only, in the reproduction by family that a breed is formed. Consanguinity alone can form, in the beginning, a bond of cohesion and connection among the descendants of the primitive families. By it, alone, they acquire that great similarity of shape and adaptation to particular ends, that great ancestral power, which they transmit to their posterity, and which, even in a commercial point of view, gives them a superior value.

If it be permitted me for this purpose to select an example within our reach among the bovine races, I would say that, in Nivernais the celebrated Charollaise breed of cattle, only a few years ago, was diffuse, without uniformity, and without commercial value. The idea of classifying it by means of a Herd-book was no sooner put in practice than good crossings, being all made with system, no longer lost their significance. The breed has visibly improved, and, at present, it has acquired a value which gives it a rank immediately after the Cotentin.

The Stud-book might be established, as we have indicated above, by inscribing therein all the stallions and mares which had received prizes for years back, continuing this operation for a dozen years to come, and adding therein also the animals which had not taken prizes or had not been shown in the fairs, but which public attention had classed among the number of types valuable on account of the beauty and sureness of their reproduction.

Parallel to the mode of improvement which I have already shown, (Chapter 1st, Part Second), and which has as its agents the members of the Council-boards and the district members of each canton, there might be formed, as a means of embracing all, a great annual Department Fair, to be held alternately in the best towns of Perche at the time of the fairs which attract the most people; in Orne, at Mortagne and Alençon; at Chartres, Nogent-le-Rotrou, and Chateaudun, for Eure and Loir; at Vendôme and Montdoubleau for the department of Loir and Cher. The departments of the Cote-d'Or, Nievre, and Youne, which possess the best Percheron stallions, might likewise enter into the association of the Percheron Stud-book, for which they have all the elements.

This book would give increased value to the breed, as is easily understood, for it is the surest of all the means of improvement and perpetuation of valuable qualities. It would drive off, forever, the defective stallions, and those corrupted with hereditary blemishes, as well as those coming from tainted families, which, I feel sure, would be refused a record in its pages. The prices of colts would likewise gain by this measure, the effect being a powerful impulse given to breeding. But it would be necessary to be very careful about ever admitting any foreign blood, in order that the recorded herds might accumulate more and more an ancestral force.

The Stud-book would offer still another advantage, that of permitting us to find again the good types, should Perche some day, in consequence of bad crossings, or from want of judgment, deviate from the true way. In fact, desire of gaining too much and of enjoying too fast at present tempts every body into innovations. Our age, so eager to enjoy, and so quick in all enterprises, has no longer the patience to wait for the improvements that time and study can alone confirm and solidly establish. It wants things off-hand, and for this it is often satisfied with adulterated products; hence, these injudicious crossings; hence, this mania for mixing together without discernment—a mania which threatens to destroy our valuable national breeds.

In the midst of all this, the opposition of the army, of the government stud-stables, and of the trade in heavy horses, bring forth new complications. The army, neither occupied in breeding nor raising, and naturally remaining beyond the consequences it causes, encourages these crossings, obtaining thereby, more rapidly, the horses it needs. But how many of the horses bred by these means are not only unfit for army service, but also unfit for any service! Indeed, with a blood stallion and a common mare, if at the first crossing, among the thin-flanked, imperfect ones, there happen to be a passable horse, good, and with a certain degree of style, ordinarily all progress ends there. For, by the use of the latter as a reproducer, an animal ungainly and without value will most certainly be the result, except by chance. The races of the south affiliate with the Arab, and those of the north with the English;

4

but the English, by the infusion of his blood, destroys the race of the south.   This mode of crossing tends, then, to cause our old French races to disappear.

At the government studs, with elevated views, and with a disinterestedness to which all delight in rendering full justice and homage, they constantly encourage the crossings in which they see the realization of their views.   They offer rewards, the most powerful of all incentives—giving but very modest prizes to the heavy horses, proscribing the light coats, and reserving their encouragement for the light horses of dark colors.

As for the trade, it adopts but slightly the views of the army and the government stables, and it gives its money to what has remained outside of these impulses.

With the Stud-book we will be able, without giving offence, to satisfy the army, the stud-stables, and the trade —the army and the stud-stables, which want the light, stylish, dark-skinned horse ; the trade—omnibuses, consumption of the large cities, and agriculture—which require weight, vigor, action, honesty, docility, and endurance.

The Stud-book will furnish the means of finding types fit for all services.   But the breeders will divide themselves into two opposite parties.   Those who wish the dark-skinned, light horse, will breed him on the uplands and in the more barren districts.   The others, in the rich, fertile, and abundant meadows, with a more nutritious food, will apply themselves to the opposite type.

Each will work in his own sphere ; the profits, losses, successes, and failures, will soon be summed up, and will soon become, on both sides, the object of minute comparisons.   If the light horse produce the most profit, his empire will soon extend over the domain of the heavy one.

But if, on the day of reaction, it be recognized that this crossing is incapable of ever making a good omnibus, a good shaft, or a good team horse ; if the crossed breed be set aside for the primitive horse ; and if it come about that the Percheron of pure race is better paid for, the fashion will soon return to him. There will the utility of the Stud-book be felt, for it will be by means of the families preserved authentically pure, in the cantons which had chosen them, that it will alone become possible to remold a race, compromised in a moment of hasty judgment, and render it plentiful upon the market.

It would suffice to bring together these types, and encourage the start in order to reëstablish Perche in all her glory. They might even, in the end, bring back to a good condition the lanky race that a better system, a more abundant nourishment, and more appropriate classification, would be called on to restore to its primitive form. Some generations would suffice to restore to it that homogeneousness that it formerly possessed, when the post-service required of it its vigorous and swift mail-coach horses.

In summing up, the Stud-book seems to me a useful agent in a triple point of view, namely: in the preservation, perfection, and restoration of the Percheron breed.

RECAPITULATION.

Preserve the Percheron race as pure as possible from all mixture not perfectly homogeneous ; respect all its varieties due to the districts where they have been bred and raised ; improve by crossing the best types of the country, and in such a manner as to correct defects, while preserving intact qualities and character.

If it be necessary to give more style to the action, and more richness to the blood, ask these qualities of the Arab, which has the privilege of imparting style and tone, while preserving weight, hardihood, vigor, and docility. The Arabian is kind, intélligent, reliable, laborious, and easily kept.

If, in obedience to urgent considerations, and in the absence of oriental horses, it becomes necessary to have recourse to English blood, choose quarter-bred stallions—at the most half-bred—but of an ancient race, and well-confirmed, with a well-opened and expressive eye, fine action, high spirit, and especially a total absence of irritability, and with all the appearances of honesty and aptitude for work.

For the innate defects of the English, generally impressible, susceptible, and unintelligent, cannot be too carefully guarded against. Delicate, a great eater, and requiring great care, he must, if honest, be well worked; if not, he pays ill his cost, and robs the hand which nourishes him. He should always be selected from a working family, and be himself a free worker. He who wishes to embark in horse-breeding will avoid more than one shoal by observing these simple considerations.

The delicate English horse, fond of his manger, bearing but little continuous and monotonous work, requiring of those that have charge of him tact, mildness, and an advanced equestrian education, is the horse of the rich man, and the man of pleasure, of the lover of the turf and chase, and of the wealthy farmer, who looks more to the beauty of his stock than to the quantity of its work.

The Arabian, sober, energetic, and laborious, is the horse for the small proprietor, the soldier, and the laborer. He is the wealth of the poorer and less improved countries.

The draft-horse is only suited to the farmer, and his size should be adapted not only to the district in which he is to be used, but also to the standard of cultivation of the country, and to the means of the person requiring his services. He may be improved, may be a trotter, and may be more stylish, but should always be adapted to the means of the breeder, and to the richness of the country. A large and fine animal would only vegetate in the hands of a person whose land is scarcely sufficient to support his family. He should only be owned by the wealthy farmer. And, on the other side, the latter should never raise his eyes to the blood horse, which should be left to those who have been a long time accustomed to the risks inseparable from his breeding and training.

A final word will make my thoughts better understood.

I desire to speak of the financial question, which is every thing in breeding and in agriculture. The best and the only manner of considering this is to compare the breeder at the start, at the beginning of his career, and when his career is ended, to verify the results. This operation is nothing short of a settlement of accounts.

In my travels I became acquainted with two neighboring districts. One was rich, fertile, and productive, eminently suited to breeding superior fancy horses. But they were poorly raised therein; the farmers disdained rearing horses suited to the soil, and the horses they did breed, already bad from the very start, were raised in idleness, and poorly fed, on account of their earning nothing. The other district was poor, and the soil produced only what could be wrested from it by force. However, by dint of labor, agriculture flourished. The horse, chosen with care, suited the country, worked well, and all prospered.

The fancy struck me, to compare the settlements of estates in these two districts, and here are the results of this examination:

In the first district, the breeders all commenced and entered upon their career with capital. Notwithstanding this, 18 out of 20 died over head and ears in debt.

In the second, they were almost all former servants or farm hands, possessing only their savings, with which to establish themselves. In spite of these difficult beginnings, 17 out of 20 left fortunes to their children, who, the reverse of the children of the former, were early accustomed to labor and to a regular life. It is useless to say that in these examples I always excepted the cases where trade, to carry on its business, sheltered itself under the cloak of the breeder; for this does not constitute breeding any more than the trade in bread-stuffs carried on in a farm-house constitutes agriculture.

Finally I would call the attention of the Percheron farmer to two suggestions. Suppose the supply of horses from the departments of Orne, Eure and Loir, Loir and Cher, Eure and Sarthe, and from the district of Mortagne, now amounting to about sixty thousand head, should outrun the demand of the omnibuses and wagons; the remedy for this would be to aim at greater style and beauty, at the same time preserving the qualities required by the omnibuses and express companies. We would thus create another outlet for our stock, through the demands of the dealers in fancy horses, and the consumption of the army, and bring the Percheron race very near to perfection.

No disappointment need be feared in crossing the Percheron with a foreign stallion, either a heavy Arabian, a strong, well-bred Merlerault, or a dark colored Norfolk, on the express condition that this stallion should be selected with care, and be of the best stock of his breed. The Arabian can be placed everywhere, both on poor land and in the hilly districts; where the progeny of the other stallions would not thrive, his will succeed well. The get of the Merlerault, and of the English horses especially, require the most fertile and the best cultivated districts.

If the results of these crossings, male or female, be successful, they may be well employed in breeding, and, after some generations, in the districts where breeding is carried on with care, they may become the starting point of a choice stock. Commencing with the qualities of good and substantial post-horses, the Percheron could be elevated to the dignity of the carriage-horse, and in other less fertile localities to staunch and compact hunters.

Those showing no improvement, (too many of which

are met with) would find a market open to them in the trade, among the moderately rich, and in the army, especially in the artillery. The males, when castrated at an early age, would be more·acceptable to the trade, and, while ceasing to dishonor the privileged class and the class destined for reproduction, could be used for numerous purposes. For the gray horse the outlets are necessarily more limited. When the omnibuses and teamsters have taken their complement of 6,000 or 7,000 horses, and when the foreigner has gathered up his 600 or 700 choice specimens, there no longer remains a sufficient demand for the second-rate stock.

As there now exist neither diligences, couriers, mail nor post-coaches, for which the gray Percheron was formerly required for the night road service, there is no longer any imperious reason for preserving his old coat; henceforth he may be bay or dark colored. And, provided he becomes so by the aid of a dark-coated Arabian, or a heavy, well-bred Merlerault, or by a fine specimen of a Norfolk, the type of his race, I see therein no inconvenience.

When steam ·machines, to supply the hands which are wanting, will plow our fields and perform the hardest work, we will have no longer to regret that our Percheron laborers have not the gray color which possessed the property of turning the scorching rays of the sun. One of our greatest writers, one of our lights in equestrian science, has, however, written :

"The use of stallions of mixed blood, borrowed from foreign races, left but regrets in Perche. It has produced vices of disposition and blemishes which did not belong to the Percheron horse, and has given him in exchange no good quality. It has disturbed the structure of the progeny without any gain in form or endurance."

Notwithstanding all my respect for this high authority, let me be allowed to ask him if he has ever seen the progeny, too rare it is true, of some well-chosen stallions in close affinity to Percheron blood, called *Gallipoli*, *Sandy*, and *Bayard?* Never did finer results gratify the pride of a breeder, never did trotters drag heavy diligences with more power and ease, and never did sons transmit more faithfully to their descendants the image and characters of their ancestors. Doubtless he was only shown the numerous and heterogeneous progeny of even the best full-blooded stallions *Sylvio*, *Eylau*, *Reveller*, and others by Percheron mares—crossings so surprising in their absence of affinity that I am still astonished that the thought of them ever entered a reasonable mind.

When in the absence of stallions of our own, such as we wish, I advise the use of foreign ones, I do not give this counsel blindly, but, select the types appearing to me the best adapted to the purpose, and instead of proceeding with giant strides I would pursue the work with a patient and prudent slowness.

PART III.

INFORMATION TO STRANGERS WISHING TO BUY PERCHERON HORSES.

———•———

Although I consider Perche an exceptional country for the production of good horses, I attribute to its air, to its water, and to the nutritiveness of its grasses, the admirable qualities of the animals bred therein. I am convinced that the excellent care, the wise management, exempt alike from pampering indulgence and from the harsh treatment which irritate the disposition, and from which the good teacher never departs in his intercourse with his pupils, contribute a great deal to the success of the result. Starting from this point, I think I can assert that with care and this identical management, horses can be elsewhere produced that Perche would not disown. It is, then, the recapitulation of this method and management which should be presented to the stranger desirous of raising the Percheron horse. I will tell him what the cultivator of this country does, and in doing like him, provided he make the attempt in a high, healthy district, a district with a sharp air and one often refreshed by winds, presenting some analogy to the rugged hills and the excellent grassy valleys of Perche, no doubt he will arrive at magnificent results. Several suppositions may be presented to the consideration of the stranger wishing to raise Percheron horses. Either he should buy in Perche a mare in

foal, or purchase four or five months' old colts, which he
wishes to wean in his own country, or his purchases will
be made of yearlings, or, finally, he will carry with him
full-grown males and females, or only one or the other
sex for the purpose of breeding.

Each one of these suppositions can be determined by the
practical knowledge of breeding, and by the study of the
methods practised in Perche, and may suggest as many
chapters. But, before undertaking anything, I will ask this
amateur if he really loves the horse, and if he admits the
qualities needed in the Percheron breeder. If he answers
in the affirmative, I will enter upon the subject. If, on
the contrary, he be not sure of himself and of the agents
that he is to employ, I might as well throw aside my pen
and not write another word.

The disposition of the Percheron breeder towards his
horses is that of a never-changing mildness; and this is
why his horse is so gentle and so docile. The Percheron
loves his horse, but not with an affection resembling that
hearty passion, that sudden blaze of regard, too explosive
to last long, of certain amateurs; he loves the horse with
an hereditary love, a family love, if I may so express it,
and the horse, on his side, loves him hereditarily. The
women and children have generally the care of the horse
while the men are in the fields. Hence the even and ami-
able temper of the horses raised under this system. The
Percheron cultivator possesses, above all, great patience
and a supreme control over himself, indispensable qualities
in training young colts, which, if treated with harsh-
ness would soon lose their heads, and become infallibly
nervously timid if subjected to violence and impatience.
Here lies the secret of good training and the art of uniting
in the horse a cool and calm temper with a decided
character. He is laborious and loves to stir the soil; hence
his practice of early working the colts, which renders
them laborious and honest. But, as he is, above all, in-

telligent and loves in a rational way, he only requires of them work in proportion to their strength, and gives them good nourishment. This management, uniting work and good food, is an admirable means of giving strength, health, and a good constitution. Finally, the Percheron inhabits a broken country, where he must constantly ascend and descend. This circumstance is most favorable in giving strength and suppleness to his shoulders, haunches, and hoofs, which, by turns, work and rest in this unparalleled district.

This portrait is not only applicable to the large proprietors and to the farmers, but to all the Percheron population. There is not a man in this district who has not been a working man, who has not raised, trained, and driven colts, and who, even in his tenderest age, when he could walk and hold a little whip, has not lived among the horses and played between their legs. It requires no searching here to find a man acquainted with the horse, a good farm hand; the first face you meet with is that of an intelligent agent, and a trustworthy one in the difficult art of training colts.

If you have such men at your disposal, undertake boldly your task; but if the proper men are wanting, forbear, for you will arrive at nothing satisfactory.

CHAPTER I.

FOOD AND BREEDING.

The stallion, in the districts inhabited by mares, is, with some rare exceptions, a " rover,"—that is to say, he visits the farms at stated periods. His standing season lasts six months, from January to July, and he generally returns four times to the same place. The foal is dropped, ordinarily, very early, and always in the stable, where it constantly remains until weaning time. The dam goes to work every day, and leaves its foal each morning, to see it again only in the middle of the day, and at night. Green clover, or other green forage, is fed, to keep up her supply of milk.

At six months the colt is weaned. If it be a filly, it remains in the canton where it was foaled, to be put to breeding when it reaches the proper age. If it be a horse colt, it is sold to the farmers of the raising districts, of which we will speak in the chapter devoted to the trade.

The stock of these districts is recruited from two sources, the southern region principally, (in the vicinity of Montdoubleau and Chateaudun,) on account of the great reputation of its mares. The cultivator desirous of rearing good colts traverses these districts as early as the month of June, and makes his choice of colts from under the dams, and out of herds of established reputation. This manner of selecting stock to raise is the most logical, as also the most expensive. It is much in favor with the farmer carrying on a large business, in the neighborhood of Mauves and Regmalard. Some cultivators of the other cantons follow his example; but not so rich as he, they have but the second choice.

The second source, and the most abundant, is the purchase of gang colts—that is to say, those which, in Perche, have not been sold during the summer; but principally those from the neighborhood of Coulie, to the north-west of Mans, and those of Lower Maine. They are brought, entirely weaned, to the fairs of Perche about the end of autumn. St. Andrew's fair at Mortagne offers a curious specimen of this operation. The farmers select from the gangs. The origin, in this case, is no longer of any account; there is neither sire nor dam to weigh down the scales; the merit is all exterior—of the individual. If this way of buying be not so dear, it is likewise not so sure, unless the purchaser be acquainted with honest dealers, accustomed to bring in only good colts.

There is but little trouble taken in weaning the colts. This passage from one period of life to another, always so serious with thoroughbred colts, takes place quite simply with the future field laborers. They wean themselves in the trip from their birthplace to their new destination. The farmers in the neighborhood of Régmalard, who ordinarily buy them very young, give a little cow's milk on their arrival, to strengthen them, and to serve as a transition; but even this method is far from universal.

The colts, when they come upon the farms, are put five or six together, pell-mell, into an indifferently ventilated stable, which receives its light through a lattice door. Their nourishment consists of a very thin mush, made of barley flour and bran, frequently renewed. The solid portion of their food is composed of dry clover and hay, with which their cribs are regularly filled.

Some farmers feed aftermath, which is sweeter; but as this is apt to load the stomach, in order to render it more easily digested, it is mixed with oat-straw.

It is very rare that these colts, changed from one district to another, often making long stages, and exposed to the inclemencies of the weather, are not attacked with strangles. Many raisers at this period have the pernicious habit of giving them some kind of grain, in order to warm them up, and cause them to throw off the disease. But this food has the fault of thickening the blood too much, and exposes them to numerous ailments.

This diet is continued until the spring, at which time the colts are given green fodder in the stable. Later, they are turned into the clover fields after the first cut, or into the meadows after they are mowed.

At eighteen months they commence their apprenticeship; passing their necks through the collar, they are harnessed to plows or wagons with horses already broken, although of an age at which, in many countries, their equals are as yet ignorant of all labor. The food, composed of clover principally, hay, millet straw, corn salad, (*Feticus*,) and cracked rye, baked in loaves, becomes from this time forth, a little more nourishing. They also commence to eat oats, but as yet, sparingly. This is not given them pure, but with the chaff—that is to say, it is not winnowed. The quantity of this food used by day is not less than $1\frac{1}{2}$ to $1\frac{3}{4}$ gallons, yielding not much more than $\frac{1}{3}$ of a gallon of oats. On the other hand, the meal and the mush are increased, to give them body and strength. At thirty months old they are still kept upon this food, in the midst of all the farm work, which they daily perform (with, however, a great deal of moderation), and in dragging very light burdens; for, truly, it is but a training, to confirm the hereditary mildness of their character, and to teach them, little by little, to become willing and fearless.

In the meanwhile the dealer, who roams constantly about among the farms, arrives. He buys and resells immediately to the farmers of Little Perche and Thimerais. More stimulating feed is given them, in consequence of more constant and harder work. This life lasts a year, and is terminated by the passage into Beauce, or the Chartres country, where their work is again increased. With the work the feed increases, and this combination leads to the perfection of the horse.

It is at this time that the horses, having attained their maturity, and the maximum of their strength, are bought for Paris, whither they are called by relentless labor, which they are enabled to endure by their unconquerable will, great muscular force, energy, and courage.

"This mode of training," to borrow the words of a noted breeder, "represents the division of labor, which gives such happy results in the manufactories, and its advantages cannot be well appreciated, except by those who, having raised horses, know what embarrassment an assemblage of colts of all sizes and ages produces. Unfortunately it would be very difficult to introduce this excellent custom elsewhere, which has probably existed for ages in Perche without the knowledge of its source."

The colts destined for breeding are generally devoted to this purpose at the age of two years, and continue, on an average, until they have attained the age of four. I speak of Little Perche, for in Great Perche, since the foundation of the Equestrian Society, the seat of which is at Chateaudun, and which extends its action to quite a distance, the covering is done by adult stallions. At four, they are sold either to Paris, or to foreigners, should their merit render them worthy of such a choice.

This total emigration of the male colts at the age of six months, renders it very difficult to procure good stallions of this breed. From Great Perche they are scattered among the trade, often before the age of a sure selection. When they are sought after in Perche, they are no longer to be found; they must then be followed and hunted up on the Beauce farms, and this pursuit is extremely difficult. It, however, offers greater chances of success than the Chartres market, where the greatest number of mature Percheron horses are to be found.

As for the fillies, their experience is the same as that of the colts, with this single difference that their life is exempt from migration. They are raised in the region in which they are foaled. They work from a very early period, bear two or three colts, and then disappear, like the males, in the vortex of consumption. For, beyond some exceptional cases and remarkable productions, it is rare that they grow old upon the farm. The farmer, in order to lose nothing of their value, sends them off at the age of five, six, and seven years. It would be a happy thing, as we have already said, if sufficient inducements in the way of prizes could be offered to retain the fine breeding mares upon the soil, and put an end to this custom, so inimical to progress.

The farmers who have pasture grounds, as in the environs of Regmalard, make use of them for raising their colts, as is done in Merlerault and in the Auge Valley. Instead of letting them loose in the fields, they are sent to pasture.

The hay of the valleys is good, but insufficient for the supply of the farms; the deficit is made up by the use of artificial fodders, in which clover enters for three-quarters; the remainder is composed of fenugreek, lucern, and some roots. Millet, or barley and oat straw are also given as food, and in certain cantons they are stacked in alternate layers with the meadow grass, in order to give them the odor and fragrance of hay—an ingenious method of making an unattractive food acceptable.

The stables, although much better than formerly, in the good old times of the race, still leave a great deal to be desired. They are not furnished with stalls, but the horses are tied alongside of one another without any separation. But such is the gentleness of character of this breed that an accident was never heard of.

The whole of the management which we have just described has a marked tendency towards constantly enlarging the horse at the expense of his nervous system.

This diet, completely out of place in a mild, grain producing country, has reason for existing in Perche, and the Percheron cultivator knows too well what he does in employing it, not to have understood this. The climate and the products of Perche, the air and the water, affect too exclusively the nervous system not to require being constantly combatted.

For this I desire to take an example in the whole animal kingdom stocking this country. Everybody to-day well knows the influence of climate upon animals. No one

now any longer doubts that it is to the sharp and healthy
air of the Percheron country, to its elevated hills, and to
its atmosphere constantly renewed by the powerful ven-
tilators of its valleys and forests, that this country owes
the eminent qualities of its fine race of horses, which has
won for it the right of displaying this significant title:
"Perche, the land of good horses." Everything surround-
ing us inclines us to adopt this opinion. The domestic
animals brought here are transformed in a short time by
the contact of the air breathed and the nourishment
furnished. The marked types of the Billot and Crêve-
cœur fowls are no sooner brought here than at the first
generation a total change is effected in their looks. From
the second generation it is difficult to recognize them in
the thin, lean, and nervously formed fowl, with a wild
look, and always ready to take wing.

The bovine race of Perche is also far inferior to the improved race. It is the opposite of the kind prized nowa-
days, the race which is mild, lymphatic, and short-legged,
always inclined to fat, and having in its bony frame only
just enough to serve it for its locomotion, forming a
quadrilateral of flesh, mounted on four small legs, a rump
bending with its haunches, a broad, smooth back, and a
low brisket. Its horns, which are seemingly useless in a
country from which man has driven out the wild beasts,
fall overlapping one another, like a useless ornament, upon
the head.

Such is not the Percheron breed of cattle; on the contrary it is dry and bony, of a nervous temperament, long
legs, angular haunches, contracted chest, lank thigh, and thin
neck, with a long, thin head. Two long horns of a greenish-
white stand up in the air, always threatening as in a savage
country, infested with dangerous animals. An expressive
word designates them fully: a cattle dealer will tell you
they are "staggy," and will pass on without bestowing upon
them a glance. They are hardly fit for quick fattening,

and are recognized without trouble by their color, which in terms of the trade is said to be " *a little weak*," and by their skin, which is dry and harsh. The dealers appropriately express their condition by "*no good points.*" The bulls, especially, are tough, with big horns, bony limbs, large joints, an ugly head, and the whole difficult to fatten, which well entitles them to the full application of the epithet " *boorish beasts*," invented to express animals of inferior quality.

It is in vain that Maine, the district which joins it, has given to Perche its race of cattle; they have degenerated, have become taller, lanker, less easy to fatten, and have preserved no trace of the fine head and the good fore-quarters that are to be found in Maine. In vain has Normandy poured out a generous blood. The Norman type hardly appears; it is degenerated and entirely loses the agreeable color, fine head, good limbs, white horns, and other good points.

For several years, the fashion of crossing with the Cotentin race has become universal, and continues to make rapid progress. From the second generation, nevertheless, there remains almost nothing in the conformation and in the quality of the stock to show the cross. It is only by dint of always crossing with the Cotentin that Perche has been able to make for itself her present passable stock.

The sheep, sufficiently delicate for the table, are small, and form a degenerate and nameless mixture of the breeds of Maine, Caux, and Trennes, crossed for several years back with the Merino. They present the same conditions as the horned animals. Like them, they are difficult to fatten and are not lymphatic, notwithstanding the frequent importations of the heavier and fleshier breeds.

Such predispositions can only come from the soil, and the constant sway of the nervous over the lymphatic system produces all the qualities of the Percheron horse. This is why tradition has painted such a seductive picture of his construction and qualities. This is why the old inhabitants, who had seen that fine breed before its degeneration, speak of it with so much warmth. This is why, notwithstanding the incredible crossings, it has withstood such mixtures. And this is why it is always energetic, in spite of the diluted nourishment without tonic properties which is given it, and which would be enough to bastardize a race with characteristics less fixed and permanent.

Let us, however, beware of utterly condemning the management of the breeders, and let us not entangle, with an imprudent hand, the threads of his traditions. The horse is his sole fortune, and in the raising of this aid of his agricultural labors, he gains to-day his livelihood. His management has a fixed end to which he always tends with an incredible perseverance, and that is to increase the size of his horses without prejudice to their good qualities.

Now that the country is covered with excellent roads and highways; that railways have accustomed us to great speed; that diligences and mail-coaches are forever gone; that the *stylish* carriage horse, the hunter, and the half-blood, have reached great perfection, the rôle of the Percheron is completely changed. He is no longer the hunter, the saddle-horse, nor the motive power of heavy wagons over new and broken roads; he remains exclusively both the quick and mettlesome draft-horse, and the heavy burden and express wagon horse. He must possess superior strength, speed, docility, temper, and honesty, and a complete absence of irritability. It is for this reason that after having listened to enthusiastic advisers, and allowed himself to be led astray by men too eager to enjoy the result of their ideas, he to-day is no longer to be cajoled by the solicitations of the amateurs of foreign blood. The Percheron cultivator does not wish even a single drop of it, and exerts himself exclusively in producing heavy horses. Encouraged in this way by the dealers of

all countries, paying excessively high prices for the big
and heavy Percheron horse, while leaving upon his hands,
without the offer of a farthing, the horse in which a few
drops of "blood" can be perceived, he has spread his sails
and stretched them boldly to catch the breeze of the day.

We shall carefully avoid following the example of
numerous famous doctors, the display of our little bundle
of receipts. Let it be, however, permitted us to touch
again slightly upon the question in expressing the fear
that, should he not take care, the breeder of heavy horses
will in the end render them too heavy and weighty.
Stallions having a small touch of blood, well applied, and
sufficiently latent not to excite mistrust, having action,
good limbs, strong loins, and deep chest, are indispensable
for warming up the Percheron blood and giving it tone.
Look at *Sandy*, and afterwards at *Collin, Bayard*, and
some others whose influence was immense. Their progeny,
magnificent in every respect, did not show too much blood
in their exterior, but revealed it vigorously by action and
high spirit. The crosses which have best succeeded with
the Percheron are undoubtedly, as shown by numerous
examples, those derived themselves from an oriental cross.
This fact, which clearly proves that the Percheron race
has a great affinity with the race of the desert, should not
be neglected in foreign alliances.

As for the English alliances, these have not given as
yet all the results promised ; but from this nothing must
be inferred against new trials. Too much blood had constantly been used, and consequently the end was missed
by wishing to proceed too rapidly.

Little blood, at first, but blood well chosen, from the
Norfolk race, blood patiently infused into Percheron veins,
is the means of triumphing over old prejudices and open-
ing to this country an extensive and successful future.

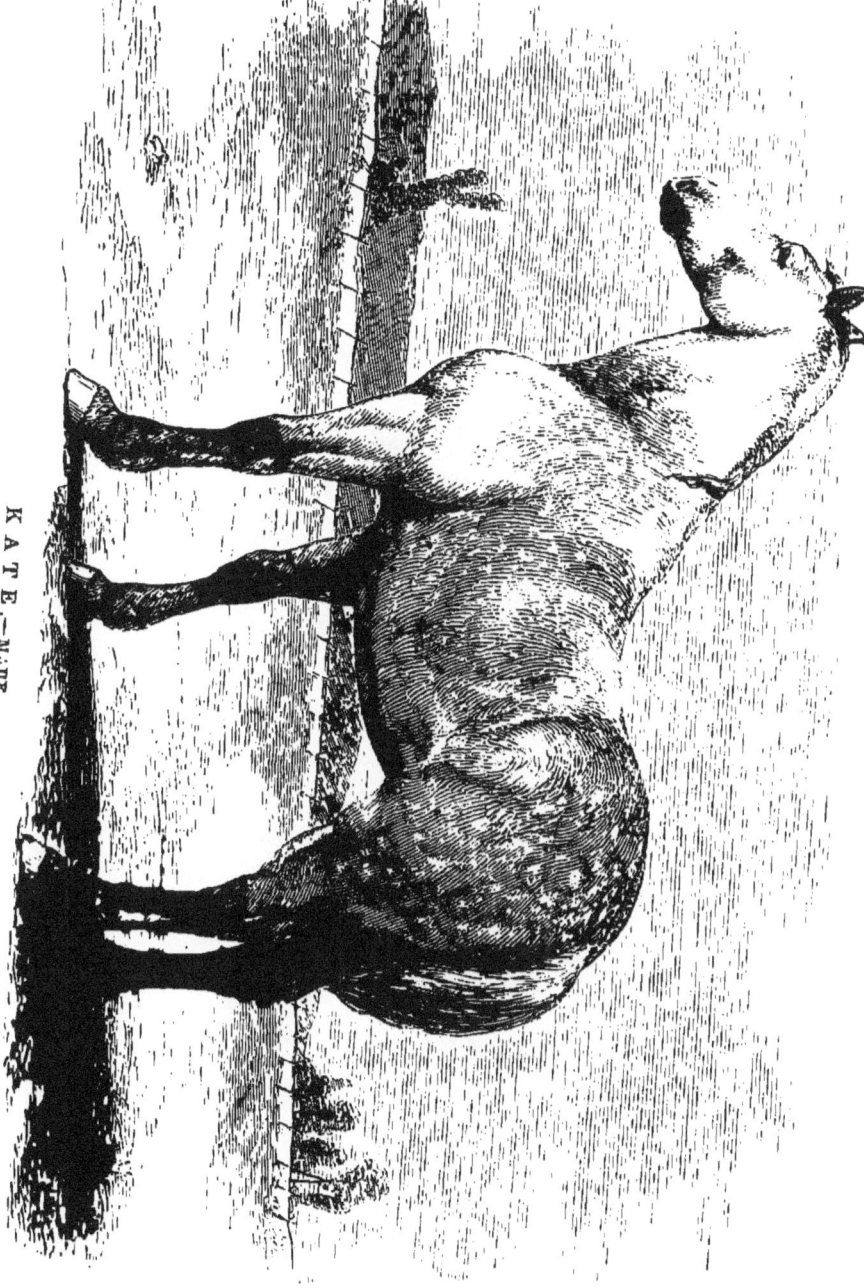

KATE.—MARE.

CHAPTER II.

TRADE. — GLANCE AT THE MOST CELEBRATED BREEDING PLACES.

The good horses are generally bought upon the farms, and among these the dealers are constantly roaming. The trade of the whole of France, and the numerous and intelligent amateurs from abroad, visit them carefully, beating the country and searching it in all its farthest corners. Still, notwithstanding the purchases there made, the fairs are not wanting in numerous and good animals. We will, like these strangers, run over the best breeding places.

As an equine country, "Perche, the land of good horses," is divided into three very distinct districts.

That in which the colts are foaled—stocked exclusively with mares and fillies ;

The district in which the male colts are weaned and raised ;

And that in which they are brought to perfection—a privilege which it shares with Beauce and the Chartres country which it bounds.

All the territory north, west, and south, of the district of Mortagne (Orne) comprising the cantons of Moulins, Bazoche, Perveuchères,.Bellesme, Theil, and part of Nocé, possesses breeding mares as well as fillies. In Sarthe, the canton of Montmirail; those of Montdoubleau and Droué in Loir-and-Cher ; those of Alluye, Bazoche, Cloyes, Authon, Brou, and Nogent-le-Rotrou, in Eure-and-Loir, are likewise centers where only fillies and breeding mares are to be met with. Courtalain, on the south border, is also celebrated for this specialty.

The raising of male-colts occupies all the east, center, and north of the district of Mortagne—that is to say, the cantons of Mortagne, Tourouvre, Lougny, Regmalard, and part of Nocé. This division, however, is not always distinctly marked upon the borders. The parishes upon the confines of each district, such as Bazoches, Courgeoust, Pin, Saint-Ouen, Nocé, Berdluis, etc., have farms stocked exclusively with fillies, whilst others possess only stallion colts.

The region for the mares is itself divided into two cantons: that of the north and that of the south. The southern is the most renowned, inasmuch as its mares pass for having retained the characters of the old Percheron race more closely. It comprises the cantons outside the district of Mortagne. Montdoubleau is the capital.

The northern, enclosed in the district of Mortagne, counts three very distinct varieties, namely:

The pure Percheron races in the south, and in the canton of Bazoches; in the west, in the parishes which border on Mesle-sur-Sarthe, mares possessing in various degrees some of English blood, got from the government stud of Mesle-sur-Sarthe, which is composed exclusively of thoroughbred stallions; the canton of Moulins, in the north, nourishes another high-spirited variety, endowed with excellent action, but deficient in height. Accordingly it is more valued for furnishing good horses for service than for furnishing ameliorating types.

The best centers for stallion colts are: Regmalard, which is, if I may so say, the principal place for good stallions; Mauves, which furnished, thirty years ago, the famous stallion Jean-le-Blanc, of M. Miard. For fillies, Villers-en-Ouche, which stocked this country with magnificent Percheron mares; Verrieres, Corbon, Comblot, Courgeou, Loisail, Reveillon and Villiers.

As for the rest of Perche, it supplies Beauce and the Chartres country, on account of the great similarity existing between them. A country of transition, it buys colts to plow the fields, keeps them only a year, and sells them grown to the cultivators of Beauce, to be sent to

Paris after a sojourn of a year or so upon their farms. The environs of Courville—Chateauneuf, Brézolles, La Loupe, Champroud, Thiron, Pontgouin, Verneuil, etc.— are celebrated for the taste of its farmers for fine horses. Illiers, which formerly possessed this specialty, has occupied itself for several years in weaning colts.

CHAPTER III.

SPEED AND BOTTOM OF THE PERCHERON HORSE.

We have said that one of the distinctive qualities of the Percheron horse, and one which has won for him universal esteem, was fast trotting while drawing a heavy load. It would be, however, an error to suppose that this faculty of fast trotting puts him on a level with the blood-horse. The latter draws little, it is true; but he has a long stride, and, as regards mere speed, he beats the Percheron out and out. For the presence upon the turf of such horses as *Décidée* and *Sarah*, who have trotted against blood-horses of the first order, sometimes honorably beaten and more often victorious, the presence, I say, of such horses, is but a happy and rare exception.

The specialty of the Percheron, quick draft, has then its limits, and it is these limits that I wish to make known by means of numerous examples collected with care.

What the Percheron has done in the diligences, mail and post-coaches is known to everybody; and it is useless to repeat it. From one relay to another, never dragging less than two, and more often three thousand pounds, in hot weather and cold, and over hilly, difficult roads, he made his three leagues to the hour easily, and sometimes four; but this was the "*ne plus ultra,*" beyond which it was not reasonable to go.

What he does in the omnibuses, the world that visits Paris realizes and admires. And this is one of the principal attractions of the Percheron horse to the intelligent stranger.

It now only remains for us to follow him upon the turf and sum up the time made in the trots won by him.

The courses, for some time frequented by him, are those of Illiers, Courtalain, Montdoubleau, and Mortagne; and here he is always to be found. It is, also, indispensable to notice, in order to be strictly impartial, that these tracks, except the new one at Mortagne, finished two years ago, were only plowed fields, hard in dry weather, but cut up like a peat-bog in wet times; that the track of Mortagne, as is well known, is placed on a steep side-hill, and joins to the above defect the one of offering three steep inclines, up and down, like the roof of a house, within a distance of 3,000 feet. The horses which had done the best elsewhere failed on this track, and took a long time to make the distance. It is to this circumstance that is to be attributed the low average time, but it is this also which shows us the courage of the Percheron. When a colt of thirty months (and of these there were a number) had bravely accomplished his task and had gone two or three times around this killing track, it could be boldly predicted that there was in him the making of a staunch and valuable horse. To all this let us add, that either under saddle or in harness, the Percheron is almost always placed in an unfavorable situation. Mounted, he is put into the hands of a youth, ardent, without experience, and without calculation, who pushes him without discretion in the beginning, and is totally ignorant of the jockey's art. Harnessed, he is covered with heavy and inconvenient gear, and he drags either a big, heavy-running wagon, or a poor, low traveling-tilbury.

The following list shows the result of 196 trotting matches, officially reported upon the turf, and two trials to prove bottom, likewise certified with care, and will give an average of what the Percheron is capable of doing either upon rugged, cut-up, or hilly tracks, or upon the highways of a densely populated district.

——◦◦◦——

CHAPTER IV.

SPEED OF THE PERCHERON HORSE.

MOUNTED PERCHERONS.

1¼ MILES —— 29 RESULTS.

The best two are those of *Julie*, at Montdoubleau, in 1864, time 3 minutes 50 seconds; and of *Godius*, at the same place, in 1857, time 3 minutes 58 seconds.

The poorest two results are those of *Vidocq*, at Mortagne, 1865, time 7 minutes 37 seconds; and of *Lansquenet*, same place, in 1861, time 7 minutes 48 seconds.

The average time of 29 recorded trials is about 4 minutes 12½ seconds.

1⅝ MILES —— 31 RESULTS.

The best two are those of *Vaillante*, at Mortagne, in 1864, time 4 minutes 38 seconds; and of *Julie*, at Montdoubleau, in 1864, time 6 minutes 14 seconds.

The poorest two are those of *Mouche*, at Mortagne, in 1855, time 9 minutes 18 seconds; and of *Biche*, at Mortagne, in 1855, time 8 minutes 30 seconds.

The average time of 31 trials is about 6 minutes 40 seconds.

5

2 MILES —— 40 RESULTS.

The best two are those of *Cocotte*, at Illiers, in 1861, time 6 minutes 5½ seconds; and of *Sarah*, at the same place, in 1865, time 6 minutes 2 seconds.

The poorest two are those of *Balzane*, at Illiers, in 1859, time 9 minutes 40 seconds; and of *Renaud*, at the same place, in 1850, time 10 minutes 30 seconds.

The average time of 40 trials is about 7 minutes 20 seconds.

2½ MILES —— 65 RESULTS.

The best two are those of *Sarah*, at Langou, in 1865, time 7 minutes 35 seconds; and of the same at Mortagne, in 1865, time 7 minutes 40 seconds.

The poorest two are those of *Marmotte*, at Mortagne, in 1865, time 13 minutes 26 seconds; and of *Julie*, at Courtalain, in 1863, time 11 minutes 30 seconds.

The average time of 65 trials is about 9 minutes 15 seconds.

——

2⅓ miles were made at Illiers, by *Bichette*, in 1860, in 12 minutes 15 seconds.

2⅝ miles at the same place were made three times, and gave an average of 11 minutes 25 seconds.

3⅝ miles at the same place were made by *Champion*, in 1857, in 12 minutes.

HARNESSED PERCHERONS.

⅞ of a mile was trotted to harness in 1855, at Bethune, by *Grise*, in 4 minutes 2 seconds.

1¼ miles were made at Mortagne, in 1856, by *Battrape*, in 5 minutes 4 seconds.

2 MILES —— 8 RESULTS.

The best two are those of *Achille*, at Illiers, in 1865, time 7 minutes 17 seconds; and of *Julie*, at Illiers, in 1863, time 7 minutes 40½ seconds.

The poorest two are those of *Championnet*, at Illiers, 1858, time 7 minutes 53 seconds; and of *Bichette*, at Illiers, in 1849, time 8 minutes 13 seconds.

The average of eight trials is about 7 minutes 36 seconds.

2½ MILES —— 14 RESULTS.

The best two are those of *Vigoreux*, at Illiers, in 1851, time 8 minutes 30 seconds; and of *Bibi*, at Mortagne, in 1865, time 9 minutes 54 seconds.

The poorest two are those of *Bichette*, at Courtalain, in 1860, time 11 minutes 30 seconds; and of *Artagnan*, at Mortagne, in 1850, time 11 minutes 55 seconds.

2⅗ MILES —— LOADED.

Two trials were made at Rouen, by *Décidée:*

The first time in 1864, drawing 386 pounds, 2⅗ miles in 9 minutes 21 seconds; the second time, in 1865, drawing 408 pounds the same distance, 10 minutes 49 seconds.

CHAPTER V.

ENDURANCE OF THE PERCHERON HORSE.

A gray mare bred by M. Beaulavoris, at Almenesches, (Orne), in 1845, belonging to M. Montreuil, horse dealer at Alençon, performed the following match: — Harnessed to a traveling-tilbury, she started from Bernay at the same time as the mail courier from Rouen to Bordeaux, and arrived before it at Alençon, having made 55¾ miles over a hilly and difficult road, in 4 hours and 24 minutes.

This mare is still living, and now belongs to M. Buisson, hotel keeper at the sign of the White Horse, at Lées, (Orne), where she still draws the omnibus plying between the railroad station and the hotel.

A gray mare 7 years old, belonging to M. Consturier, of Fleury-sur-Andelle, (Eure), in 1864, harnessed to a tilbury, travelled 58 miles and back on two consecutive days, going at a trot and without being touched with the whip. This was over the road from Lyons-la-Foret from Pont Audemer, and back, a difficult and hilly way. The following time was made: The first day the distance was trotted in 4 hours, 1 minute, and 35 seconds; the second day, in 4 hours, 1 minute, and 30 seconds. The 13¾ last miles were made *in one hour*, although at about the 41st mile the mare was obliged to pass her stable to finish the distance.

GARDENING FOR PROFIT,

In the Market and Family Garden.

BY PETER HENDERSON.

FINELY ILLUSTRATED.

This is the first work on Market Gardening ever published in this country. Its author is well known as a market gardener of eighteen years' successful experience. In this work he has recorded this experience, and given, without reservation, the methods necessary to the profitable culture of the commercial or

MARKET GARDEN.

It is a work for which there has long been a demand, and one which will commend itself, not only to those who grow vegetables for sale, but to the cultivator of the

FAMILY GARDEN,

to whom it presents methods quite different from the old ones generally practiced. It is an ORIGINAL AND PURELY AMERICAN work, and not made up, as books on gardening too often are, by quotations from foreign authors.

Every thing is made perfectly plain, and the subject treated in all its details, from the selection of the soil to preparing the products for market.

CONTENTS.

In the last chapter, the most valuable kinds are described, and the culture proper to each is given in detail.

Sent post-paid, price $1.50.

ORANGE JUDD & CO., 245 Broadway, New-York.

NEW AND BEAUTIFUL WORK.

The Book of Evergreens.

BY

JOSIAH HOOPES, Westchester, Pa.

INCLUDING

Propagation, Cultivation, Description of Varieties, and their Adaptability to Different Situations.

THIS is a long-needed work, as in it the present state of our knowledge upon the cone-bearing plants, or Coniferæ of the botanist, is posted up. Mr. Hoopes is one of those persons rarely met with—a practical cultivator, and a man of science at the same time. While his work gives us all the Coniferæ arranged in the classification of the botanist, it at the same time treats of the experience, not only of the author, but of American cultivators generally, with this large and important family of plants.

Evergreens play so interesting a part, not only in ornamental planting, but in what may be termed economical planting, (*i. e.* hedges, screens, windbreaks, etc.,) that we are sure a work which treats of their propagation and culture, describes in both popular and scientific language the many species, and, what is of not the least importance, gives a list of the tender and unreliable ones, will be warmly welcomed by every lover of these beautiful trees.

Mr. Hoopes brings to his work a perfect enthusiasm for his subject, and is as free to condemn a plant as if he were not a nurseryman. All the latest novelties from Japan, the Northwest, etc., are noticed, and their success or failure, both in this country and in England, is recorded.

The work is abundantly illustrated with most carefully executed engravings, for the greater part from living specimens.

We must commend the conscientious care the author has shown in striving to arrive at the proper names; and doubtless much of the confusion that at present exists in respect to names among both dealers and growers, will be corrected now that they have a standard work to refer to.

Not the least interesting portion of the book is an account of the principal collections of evergreens in the country.

The work contains 435 pages, 12mo, on fine paper.

Sent post-paid. Price, $3.00.

ORANGE JUDD & CO.,
245 Broadway, New-York City.

VALUABLE AND BEAUTIFUL WORK.

HARRIS'
Insects Injurious to Vegetation.

BY THE LATE

THADDEUS WILLIAM HARRIS, M.D.

A New Edition, enlarged and improved, with additions from the author's manuscripts and original notes.
Illustrated by engravings drawn from nature under the supervision of

PROFESSOR AGASSIZ.

Edited by CHARLES L. FLINT,

Secretary of the Massachusetts State Board of Agriculture.

CONTENTS.

Published in two beautiful editions; one plain, with steel engravings, 8vo, extra cloth, $4; the other in extra cloth, beveled boards, red edges, engravings colored with great accuracy, $6.

Sent post-paid on receipt of price.

ORANGE JUDD & CO.,
245 Broadway. New-York City

AMERICAN POMOLOGY
APPLES.

By Doct. JOHN A. WARDER,

PRESIDENT OHIO POMOLOGICAL SOCIETY; VICE-PRESIDENT AMERICAN POMOLOGICAL SOCIETY.

293 ILLUSTRATIONS.

This volume has about 750 pages, the first 375 of which are de voted to the discussion of the general subjects of propagation, nur. sery culture, selection and planting, cultivation of orchards, care of fruit, insects, and the like; the remainder is occupied with descriptions of apples. With the richness of material at hand, the trouble was to decide what to leave out. It will be found that while the old and standard varieties are not neglected, the new and promising sorts, especially those of the South and West, have prominence. A list of selections for different localities by eminent orchardists is a valuable portion of the volume, while the Analytical Index or *Catalogue Raisonné*, as the French would say, is the most extended American fruit list ever published, and gives evidence of a fearful amount of labor.

CONTENTS.

Chapter   I.—INTRODUCTORY.
Chapter   II.—HISTORY OF THE APPLE.
Chapter III.—PROPAGATION.
            Buds and Cuttings—Grafting—Budding—The Nursery.
Chapter IV.—DWARFING.
Chapter   V.—DISEASES.
Chapter VI.—THE SITE FOR AN ORCHARD.
Chapter VII.—PREPARATION OF SOIL FOR AN ORCHARD.
Chapter VIII.—SELECTION AND PLANTING.
Chapter IX.—CULTURE, Etc.
Chapter   X.—PHILOSOPHY OF PRUNING.
Chapter XI.—THINNING.
Chapter XII.—RIPENING AND PRESERVING FRUITS.
Chapter XIII and XIV.—INSECTS.
Chapter XV.—CHARACTERS OF FRUITS AND THEIR VALUE—TERMS USED.
Chapter XVI.—CLASSIFICATION.
            Necessity for—Basis of—Characters—Shape—Its Regularity—Flavor—Color—Their several Values, etc. Description of Apples.
Chapter XVII.—FRUIT LISTS—CATALOGUE AND INDEX OF FRUITS.

Sent Post-Paid.   Price $3.00.

ORANGE JUDD & CO., 245 Broadway, New-York.